The Royal Pain

The Royal Pain

MARYJANICE DAVIDSON

BRAVA

KENSINGTON PUBLISHING CORP.
http://www.kensingtonbooks.com

BRAVA BOOKS are published by

Kensington Publishing Corp.
850 Third Avenue
New York, NY 10022

All Kensington titles, imprints, and distributed lines are available at special quantity discounts for bulk purchases for sales promotions, premiums, fund-raising, educational or institutional use.

Special book excerpts or customized printings can also be created to fit specific needs. For details, write or phone the office of the Kensington Special Sales Manager: Kensington Publishing Corp., 850 Third Avenue, New York, NY 10022, attn: Special Sales Department. Phone: 1-800-221-2647.

Brava and the B logo Reg. U.S. Pat. & TM Off.

ISBN 0-7582-0806-5

First Kensington Trade Paperback Printing: November 2005
10 9 8 7 6 5 4 3 2 1

Printed in the United States of America

For Julie Kathryn Gottlieb, who whines when
I don't dedicate a book to her.
Off my case, hose-face.

We are born with luck
Which is to say with gold in our mouth.
As new and smooth as a grape,
As pure as a pond in Alaska,
As good as the stem of a green bean
We are born and that ought to be enough.
—Anne Sexton, *The Evil Seekers*

Treason and murder ever kept together.
—William Shakespeare, *Henry V*

A Sheldon can do your income taxes. If you need a root canal, Sheldon's your man. But humpin' and pumpin' is not Sheldon's strong suit. It's the name. "Do it to me, Sheldon. You're an animal, Sheldon. *Ride* me, big . . . SHELdon." Doesn't work.
—Harry, *When Harry Met Sally*

Acknowledgments

Thanks again to my wonderful family, who may well recognize parts of themselves in some of these pages but too bad, I've already spent the advance.

Extra thanks to my dad, the inspiration for King Al, who once explained to me that he could never run for president because the newspapers wouldn't print "fuck" and thus he would never be properly quoted. When I got over my startlement, I realized he was right. And once again, America was cheated of a great leader, all because the papers won't print the word "fuck."

Also, thanks to Giselle, Stacy, and Jessica, who listen to my endless complaints and give excellent advice (chief of which: "Stop yer bitching").

Thanks also to my sister, Yvonne, who reminded me what a bail is for and was kind enough not to give me shit about blanking on the word.

Thanks are also due to the exalted Kate Duffy, who edits her authors as gently as a sighing kitten and promotes them as savagely as a ravenous white shark. She works too hard and her bosses should give her a raise at once.

Finally, thanks to the readers who have been asking me whatever happened to those pesky Baranovs. You got me wondering, so here we all are.

Author's Note

As with *The Royal Treatment*, I've taken liberties and, as of this writing, Alaska still is not a country. However, it is possible to kill someone with a chair and nightmares do inevitably result.

The events of this book take place twenty-two months after the wedding of His Royal Highness Prince David to Lady Christina.

Prologue

The Sitka Palace
2:32 A.M.

"Nicky, *get down!*" Alexandria's father roared, and her little brother dropped like a rock and rolled away. There was no mistaking the command in that yell; she nearly fell to the carpet herself.

There was a sound, some odd sound she should have recognized but did not, and suddenly her father was staring at the two small, feathered darts sticking out of his chest. He stared . . .

(What story tonight, Alex?)

. . . they all stared . . .

(No, hon, that one gives you nightmares.)

. . . it was all happening so fast . . .

(There's nothing to be afraid of.)

. . . and then her father . . .

(We're going to be all right now.)

. . . her father . . .

(There's no such thing as monsters.)

. . . slowly folded to the floor.

She heard another sound—the flat, smacking sound of metal hitting flesh—but she was too busy looking around, looking around for . . .

There.

"Not s'fast without y'r pea shooter, eh?" she heard some-one, Kurt? David? slur.

"Y—you have to come with me, Prince Nicholas," the monster said. He was reaching for her little brother, actu-ally *daring* to *reach* for her brother after the gross assault upon her father. "Your place is with us."

"Get the hell out of here, you traitorous piece of shit," her older brother David ordered. Alexandria agreed whole-heartedly . . . to a point. "If you leave now, our security team might not blow your head off."

Stay a while. Just a minute longer. I'll give you something to remember the Baranovs by, you prick.

"Us, sir?" her little brother, Nicholas, asked. As always in response to stress, he was overly polite.

She slipped out of one of her shoes. There was more talking, but it was background noise, it was how the ocean sounded to a starfish. Huge and irrelevant.

"My father is the true king," Nicholas said, and that she did hear. Nicholas was a child, a brave and honorable one, but too young to know it was useless to talk sense to an extremist.

"Devon!" her sister-in-law Christina shouted, and Alex-andria heard that, too, like the crack of a whip, again and again: *Devon. Devon. Devon.* "You'll never get out of here."

Never.

She caught Nicholas's gaze, saw him glance at the gun, Kurt's gun, on the floor. She shook her head but he ignored her and bent for it. Thank God, Devon was distracted by Princess Christina.

"You've fucked up, it's done."

Yes, it's done.

"You shot my daddy," Nicholas said, and the rest of them noticed what she had just seen: he had the gun. It was steady in his small hands; the butt snugly against his left palm, right index finger on the far end of the trigger guard.

Yes, you shot my daddy.

"You shot my king and my sovereign, and you hurt my friend."

Dad.

"So I'm thinking, it's only fair if I shoot you."

Don't worry, Nicky. You won't have to. I'm going to fix him. I'm going to fix everything.

"Your High—"

The last thing Devon said. Fitting that it should be proper use of a title. Part of one, anyway. Her hands had closed over the banquet chair. Wood, not metal—but she would make do. Her grip was firm, not sweaty. (The night sweats would come later, and stay forever.) She levered the chair up off the ground; it went easy, lighter than feathers.

She swung the chair sidearm

("Honey, not like that. You're throwing like a girl. Yeah, yeah, don't go all PC on me. Do it like this.")

putting every ounce of her one-fifty behind it.

The monster did not fall; he slammed against the wall. It wasn't what she was expecting at all; it was nothing like TV. Her hands and arms absorbed most of the shock of the blow and it would be days before she could raise her wrists above her shoulder.

The chair, as she had calculated, did not shatter. It was good wood, it held. But force had to go somewhere. She had been counting on it, and from the blood coming out the monster's ears, the force had gone exactly where she intended.

"There!" she said, her arms still vibrating. "That's—" Then he got up. The monster actually got up off the floor, blood dripping down his sideburns, moving steadily, not noticing he was mortally wounded. In her head, Alex screamed and screamed.

Devon brushed cake from his uniform and took the gun from Nicholas's nerveless fingers, shot her brother David . . .

(this is wrong)

shot her other brother Nicky, shot her sister-in-law Christina. Took the chair away . . .

(it's not like this)

swung . . .

(it didn't happen like this)

and the last thing she saw was the chair, descending. The last thing she knew was that she had failed. Everyone was dead and she failed.

Chapter 1

The Sitka Palace
2:42 A.M.

She didn't scream.

She never screamed.

She was cringing in her bed, bracing herself for the blow, and it took a minute or so to remember it was just the old nightmare, she had not failed, everyone was alive, she had not failed.

She had not failed.

Princess Alexandria, third in line to the Alaskan throne, pressed a hand to her mouth, hurried to the bathroom, and threw up.

Alexandria stole down the hall, took a left, nodded to an insomniac footman, and walked quietly into the nursery. But not so quietly that her sister-in-law, Christina, didn't hear.

The nursery was right next to David and Christina's bedroom, and after years of being on her own and looking over her shoulder, Christina slept about as deeply as a cat with ADD.

There was no night-nurse; there was barely a day nurse.

(Christina had the charming idea that she should raise her own daughter, which was adorable, if common.)

Knowing she had permission, Alex scooped up the sweetly sleeping baby and cuddled her against her shoulder. Dara stirred but did not awaken and Alex simply stood over the crib, holding the baby and taking comfort in her warmth, her sweet milky smell, the fineness of her baby hair, the softness of her skin.

"Another one?" Christina whispered. She didn't whisper so as not to wake Dara; the baby didn't sleep, she hibernated. But Christina didn't want to wake her husband, who had a grueling day of ribbon cutting and Chardonnay drinking and penguin counting ahead of him. "What is this, the third time this week? And it's only Tuesday."

Alex shrugged. She adored Christina, but did not discuss the dreams with her. With anyone. Well, almost anyone.

"Alex, for God's sake. You've got to get some sleep. When was the last time you got a full eight hours? Unbroken?"

Another shrug. Alex nuzzled the top of Dara's head. The baby shifted and snored on.

"Why aren't you taking the stuff Dr. Pohl prescribed? Don't shrug again or I'll pull all your long, beautiful hair out."

She snorted. "You don't scare me, you're getting slow in your old age. And you know why."

"Well, maybe I haven't bounced back from the baby as fast as I—"

"It's kind of late for jokes."

"It's kind of late for *anything*. And here you've got a perfectly good prescription for sleeping pills in your . . . oh, God, you're just like your brother! He wouldn't take a Tylenol for an amputation. You guys."

"What?"

"Come on. I get the whole 'we're a rugged band of royals

who carved a country out of the harsh wilderness' bit, but would it kill you to pop an Ambien?"

"I don't have trouble getting to sleep," she pointed out. "Just staying asleep. And I'm sorry I woke you."

Now it was Christina's turn to shrug. "It's no big deal. *I* won't have trouble getting back to sleep," she added, raising her eyebrows. She softened a bit when Alex made no reply. "Well, I normally would, too, tomorrow being the big day and all, but I didn't get a nap today and—never mind, it's boring. In fact, never mind about all that . . . listen, why don't you take her back to bed with you? That works sometimes."

Alex grinned a little. "You're just trying to sleep in."

"Well, it's a handy bonus, I must admit. Besides, the thing doesn't even start until . . . what? Noon?"

"One," she corrected. "Sounds like someone hasn't read her program."

"Great, one, even better. Hey, you just have to change her and feed her and entertain her until I wake up . . . say, eleven-ish?"

"Nine."

"Done." Christina bent forward and planted a soft kiss on the baby's head. "Luck getting some Z's. Don't squish the baby."

Offended, she said, "I would never."

"See, you'd have a better sense of humor if you were getting a couple more hours a night."

"Hush up."

"I'm just saying," Chris said, backing away.

Alex took Dara back to her room, carefully laid the baby on the left side of the bed (the bed had been pushed against the wall months ago for that express purpose), tossed all the pillows on the floor just in case, and pulled a blanket up to the middle of the baby's back. Dara snored on, oblivious.

Five minutes later, Alex was doing the same.

Chapter 2

It was like any other family event—except with royals. The Baranovs (those who had read their schedules) were assembled in one of the many side corridors, waiting.

"I can't believe," Princess Kathryn, fourth in line to the Alaskan throne, whispered, "there's hardly anybody here but the family."

Prince David, first in line to the throne, grinned. He looked more relaxed than anybody could ever recall; the general consensus was that marriage and fatherhood agreed with him immensely. He was wearing a dark gray suit with a royal blue shirt and a gray tie dotted with tiny rockhopper penguins. His shoes, thanks to a tireless staff, were shined to a high gloss. David, thanks to a royal upbringing, didn't notice. "Hey, Chris insisted. No press, no big deal, no fuss, no—you know."

"I know what she insisted on," his sister replied. Kathryn was six months away from ridding herself of the hated braces, and was the promise of truly breathtaking beauty, with the classical Baranov coloring: sinfully dark hair, enormous, crystal blue eyes. "Like I said, I just can't believe she pulled it off."

"Dad's fond of her."

"Tell me. It's like having the sister I never wanted," she added with a mock sigh.

They were standing in the left foyer of the palace chapel, where Prince Nicholas (sixth in line to the throne) quickly joined them.

"Are we ready? Is everybody here?"

"Well," David said, "the baby's not here. And Chris isn't here. And the Alexes aren't here. And Dad—"

"Cool your jets, everybody," the king said, stepping in through a side door, his majordomo, Edmund, right on his heels. "I said I'd be here, didn't I? Right? Right. So what the hell's the holdup? Can we get this over with, please? Now? Please?"

"How did you get him into that suit?" David asked, losing his usual smooth manners and gaping at his father.

"A crow bar," Edmund replied smoothly. "Are we ready to begin?"

"Well, the godparents aren't here."

"Ah." Edmund pretended to consult his program, when everyone in the room (possibly the palace) knew he'd been the one to write it. "Prince Alexander and Princess Alexandria. And where is Her Highness, Princess Dara?"

A shrill whistle burst through the air and they all looked through the foyer door, across the front of the chapel, and into the opposite door, where Christina was holding the baby and waving madly.

"She came in through the wrong door," Edmund sighed.

"She probably didn't read the—I mean, she probably didn't pay attention to—" Princess Kathryn blushed to her eyebrows, then added, "I mean, doesn't she look gorgeous? Purple is definitely her color."

"Kid looks like an eggplant with arms," the king muttered, sticking a finger under his collar and giving it the tenth wrench of the morning. When David swung around, eyebrows raised, he hastily added, "A good-looking eggplant. Jesus! Can we please get the fucking show on the road? I could be in a fishing boat right this minute."

"Don't say 'fucking' in church, Dad," Nicholas corrected, running a hand through his cap of blonde curls. He was the only child of the king who looked nothing like his father. It had caused some trouble in the past; the late queen had been known to dally with men not her husband. "We're just waiting on the Alexes. You'll be on a boat by three. Suppertime, prob'ly, at the latest."

The king wriggled in his suit coat. "I hate these things."

"We all do, Dad."

"Shush, Your Highness. Your Majesty, stop fidgeting or I shall defect instantly to America."

"Ha! That's a bluff I'll damn well call!"

"Shhhhhhhhhhh, Dad!"

"Don't shush me, you little creep, you're not too big to spank."

"I'm two inches taller than you are, Dad," Prince David explained patiently.

"Ah, tensions are running high," Princess Alexandria said, entering the foyer. She was wearing a shin-length, long-sleeved blue silk dress the exact color of her eyes. As it was a "casual" affair, no one was wearing their crowns or any royal insignia. "My timing is perfect. Has Edmund threatened to move to the States yet?"

"Aw, shaddup," the king told her.

Alex peeked into the chapel, spotting several familiar faces . . . mostly staff and a few friends of the family. For the Baranovs, a typical low-key affair. Christina had insisted and the king had agreed: Dara had the entire rest of her life to be in the spotlight. Today was for family and friends.

Alex waved to Christina, who wiggled Dara's hand back, making it look like the baby was waving. Ugh. New parents were so weird. "She came in the wrong door," she muttered to Edmund.

"Jenny couldn't get her to pay much attention to the program," Edmund muttered back. "Your Highness, if I may make so bold, are you feeling all right?"

"I'm fine, Edmund."

"You look tired."

Alex guiltily felt the dark circles under her eyes and repeated, "I'm fine."

"What the *hell* is the hold-up now?" the king bitched. "The baby's here, the parents are here, the goddamn family shrink is here"—as one, they all peeked through the foyer and waved to Dr. Pohl, seated proudly in the third row—"the godmother's here. Can we please get this damned thing started?"

"Please don't refer to my daughter's christening as a damned thing," David said mildly, hands in his pockets.

"Prince Alex is running a bit late," Edmund admitted. "In fact, I expected him ten minutes ago. Perhaps he—"

"He's missing? Alex is gone?"

"Your Highness, I'm sure it's a simple mix-up—"

"Has anyone called him? Have you called his assistant? Did anyone look for him?" Alex could hear her voice rising with hysteria, but it was like she was outside herself, watching. Unable to stop. "When was the last time someone saw him?"

The king was staring at her. Everyone was staring at her. "Whoa, kid, simmer down."

"Simmer down?" she nearly shrieked. "One of us is *gone* and I'm supposed to lie back and take it easy? What if he's been kidnapped? What if the bad guys are taking him away right now? *Why isn't anyone doing something?*"

From the other side of the chapel, Christina thrust the baby into her startled assistant's arms, and darted across, passing the altar and the masses of red and yellow tulips decorating the sanctuary. "What's the matter? What's wrong?"

"Alex is gone! Nobody can find him! He's—"

"He's right over there with me! He came in the wrong door, too, just about half a minute ago. See?" Christina yanked the princess over to the door and bellowed, "Alex!"

After a second, the princess saw her younger brother, fourth in line to the throne, wave, and hurry across, waving again to the patiently seated onlookers.

"Don't have a cow, man,
I might have overslept some
But everything's fine."

"How long do we have to suffer the haikus," Kathryn demanded, "because he lost a bet?"

"How many times do I have to tell you to cut . . . that . . . shit . . . out . . ." Odd. Everyone was tipping away from her, and now she could see Christina's face, an oval of concern directly above her, but it was receding, pulling back, and why, why, why was it so dark in here?

"I'm tired," Alex said automatically, before even opening her eyes. "I just need a nap."

"Ha!" the king said. She opened her eyes and nearly yelled; all the Baranovs were crowded around her. Dr. Pohl— the royal psychiatrist, physician, and all-around EMT—kept elbowing them back. The stethoscope had ruined the older woman's hairstyle. "You need a trank, among other things. And if you think that got you out of the ceremony, think again, missy."

"Where am I?"

"East parlor," Edmund replied. "First floor, east wing. It was the closest couch we could find, Your Highness."

Alex started to prop herself up on her elbows, only to feel Dr. Pohl grab an elbow and pull her back down. "How long since you've had a full night's sleep?"

"Last night."

"Liar," Christina said. She was cradling the baby and looking down at Alex just as anxiously as the others. Only Dara seemed unmoved; she had nodded off on her mother's shoulder, a tiny thumb corked in her mouth. "It's been months."

"It hasn't been *that* long," Alex protested. "Will someone let me up, please?"

"After the doc gets done. And Jenny's bringing a tray. Maybe you can get up after you eat every bite."

"She was worried sick," Prince Alex bragged, slicking back his already-slicked back hair with both hands. "Fainted like a teeny girl. What a big loser."

"I was not! I was just wondering where you were."

"You really did faint like a—well, a princess, I guess. If you read the fairy tales," Kathryn added.

"I did not faint! I lost my footing for a second and the rest of you overreacted."

"You passed out," Dr. Pohl corrected, putting away her stethoscope, "due to a combination of fatigue, stress, and mal-nutrition. In fact, I'd say you're at least ten pounds under your ideal weight. Why haven't you been eating?"

"For the last time, I'm *fine*. Now *take your hands off me*."

Dr. Pohl let go of her like she was hot.

"Girly-o," her father said, his eyes slits of blue and the usual smirk nowhere to be seen on his face, "sick or not, you'd better apologize or you'll be unconscious again."

"I'm sorry, Dr. Pohl," she muttered.

"It's fine, Your Highness. I'm used to being screeched at

by royalty. Oh, the things I could tell you if not for doctor-patient privilege."

"Hey!" Christina yelped.

"Besides, we can discuss that and—other things—at your appointment."

"What?" Alex cried, and nearly fell off the couch.

Chapter 3

"**E**verything is really fine," Alexandria said, looking Dr. Pohl straight in the eye with as open and honest a gaze as had ever been on a face.

"With all due respect, Your Highness, you're full of shit."

"You sounded exactly like Princess Christina when you said that," she commented. "I must protest. How about a little respect for a member of the royal family?"

"How about a little respect for me?" Dr. Pohl replied quietly. She was an attractive, pale woman in her early sixties, with the curly white hair of a cherub and the piercing intellect of a Nobel Prize winner. Which she was. "It's quite obvious you aren't sleeping well. It was obvious before yesterday's incident."

"At least we got the ceremony done. Thank God the press wasn't there anymore."

"Yes, that's exactly the thing we should be worrying about right now. You're a beautiful woman, Princess Alexandria, but you've got bags under your eyes the size of tea cups."

"Partying," she suggested. "The wild royal lifestyle."

"Nice try, but you weren't anywhere in that issue of *People*."

Alex shrugged and looked around the large office. "It's not a problem for me. It's just . . . how things are now."

"I disagree."

"There *is* something I've been meaning to discuss with you."

Dr. Pohl raised white eyebrows.

"It might seem personal."

"Try me, Your Highness."

"I've been trying to figure out how to bring it up for months."

Dr. Pohl leaned forward. "You're safe here, Princess. You can discuss anything with me."

"What's with all the ducks?" There were pictures of mallards on the wall, wood duck statues, antique painted duck decoys, pinheads, spoonbills, and mergansers. *Two* framed duck prints from America. "I'm having waterfowl overload. Is it a special thing with you? Were you raised by mallards?"

Dr. Pohl settled back, admirably masking her sigh. She ran a hand through her white curls, adjusted her glasses, and put her pencil down. "You're changing the subject, Your Highness. Not surprising, given what happened yesterday, but not helpful, either."

"Well, I can if I want. I can talk about anything in here I want. I'm *safe*, remember?"

"You say that like you don't believe it."

She looked away. "Like I said, I can change the subject to whatever I want." She drummed her fingers on the arm of the chair, striving not to sound like a spoiled palace brat, and failing. "Current events. Waterfowl. The state of the Union. Prince William's upcoming marriage, which my dad actually thinks he'll be invited to. My niece. She's brilliant, you know."

"So you've said. Your Highness—"

"She's already talking and she's only one."

"Yes, Your—"

"She's practically toilet training herself and she's only one. Isn't that amazing? Don't you think that's amazing?"

"Fortunately, she won't ever have to worry about Devon."

Alex felt herself tighten. "That's a little obvious for a supposedly subtle analyst, isn't it?"

"I suppose."

"And there's always a Devon," she said bitterly. "Always."

"So your niece isn't safe? Your brother? Your father? If someone turns up late, they've been kidnapped?"

"Look, I overreacted yesterday, okay? Let's move on."

"You're not," Dr. Pohl said quietly, "or we would."

"B-besides, when has safety ever been a guarantee? For anyone, never mind someone in the public eye? Even for the good guys? My family didn't take this country from Russia by being nice. I'm sure felony assault was involved."

"So this is how it's *supposed* to be? You're a closed-off wreck who can't sleep because people aren't nice?"

"But my family's okay for now. If that's the trade-off, I'll take it."

"Princess Alexandria, it wasn't a deal." Dr. Pohl was leaning forward, her gaze so compassionate Alex had to look away again. "In fact, it's *not* a trade-off. Why shouldn't your family be alive and well—all respect to your late mother, the queen—and why shouldn't you have a happy and fulfilling life?"

"Well, for one thing, if I did, you'd be out of business."

"Hardly," she muttered. "Your sister-in-law keeps me on my toes." Then, louder, "How is the medication working for you?"

"Fine."

"It's amazing," Dr. Pohl said, amused. "You look like a perfect angel when you lie."

"Thanks."

"But I think we should try to make some kind of progress."

"Why?"

"Your Highness."

"What?"

"Your Highness."

"None of this is *my* idea." Alex crossed her arms over her chest and jiggled a foot up and down. "Have you seen my schedule? I've got other things to do. Like I said, this wasn't my idea. Blame my father, the big hen."

"I think it's safe to say I have never heard the king referred to as a chicken. Your Highness, in all seriousness, I can't help you if you won't let me."

"Then it sounds like we're done," she said, cheering up.

"Sit back down, Your Nice Tryness."

Glaring at the duck pencil sharpener, she did. She wondered if Congress would give her the power to have Dr. Pohl beheaded. Or at least suspended.

"Have you given any more thought to my suggestion?"

"No." This was another lie. Some nights, it was all she thought about. But ultimately . . . "It'd be like running away."

"I disagree, Your Highness."

"Of course you do. By the way, you should return that blouse. Babyshit tan is not a good color for you."

"Your transparent attempt to pick a fight about my admittedly eclectic wardrobe so we get off the subject won't work."

"Whatever you say, cotton ball."

"There's nothing wrong with trying something new, getting a little perspective. You'll be doing good work and at the same time, if you got out of the country for a while, it could do you a world of good. And since your brother can't go, it seems almost . . . fortuitous."

"Everything I need is right here."

"You don't have to stay to keep an eye on them, Alexandria."

And Alexandria, whose mother had been taken from her when she was still a child, and whose father had recently escaped death, put her head in her hands and wept.

Chapter 4

"**I** guess I'm confused," Princess Christina said.

"Then it must be Wednesday," Alex replied, not looking up from her travel itinerary.

"Ha, ha, Princess Sarcasto. Look, don't get me wrong, I think a change of scenery is just the thing. Just exactly the right thing. God knows it always cheered *me* up."

"Do you miss working for the cruise line?"

"No," Christina replied shortly. "And don't change the subject. You're not a marine biologist. You're not even—I mean, your specialty is—okay, this is kind of embarrassing, I'm trying to remember, I'm sure I read about this a couple of years ago—what *did* you do in college?"

"I have a degree in Nursing."

"Oh. Right. Well, good for you. But you're not going to a new hospital, right? I guess I'm saying, what's the point of you going along on this little joyride?"

"Other than your sinister plan to remove me from the palace so you can further destroy royal protocol?"

"Yeah, besides that."

"Working on Alaskan/American relations."

"But America and Alaska get along."

"Yes. And it's like any relationship. It needs constant tending. Such tending is part of our job—your job, too, I might add. So I'll go along and smile big and answer questions and oversee funds and smash champagne bottles on things. It's a fluff trip. This looks fine, Jenny." Alex scribbled her initials on the bottom of the pages and handed it back to the protocol officer.

"I'll finalize the preps at once, Your Highness."

"Jenny, my God! Are those *slacks?*" Christina, frozen in the act of popping a grape into her mouth, gaped.

The protocol officer, a woman Alex privately thought was an astonishingly efficient sloe-eyed beauty, blushed to her eyebrows. "I was taking Your Highness's advice, but if Your Highness feels I am dressed inappropriately for palace duty—"

"Which one of us Highnesses are you talking to? And calm down, I was only teasing. Grape? Look, it's okay. I'm sorry I even said anything, *please* relax." Christina bullied the smaller brunette into a chair. "Breathe, okay? Hey, you look great. Doesn't she look great, Alex?"

"You look great, Jenny," she repeated obediently, using all of her poker experience not to smile. Jenny really *did* look a little stressed . . . but then, she always did. Palace life was not without anxiety, no matter what the job or title. "I *like* the pants."

"Thank you, Highness."

"You should wear green all the time," Christina commented. The moment she released the other woman's elbow, Jenny sprang back to her feet. "It makes your eyes look even bigger and darker. And you should take tranquilizers. All the time."

"If you'd leave her alone, she wouldn't need the tranks," Alex commented, picking up *The Palace Poop*, the in-house newsletter advising everyone from the reigning king down to the groundskeepers of birthdays, anniversaries, scheduled softball games, and royal comings and goings. The newsletter had been Christina's idea. "Dad *told* you to quit needling the officers."

"What, 'needling'? I'm just trying to get everyone to lighten up around here. Which is not very damned easy, by the way. I mean, look at you. All stiff and starched and dressed to the nines to eat pudding. And not even chocolate pudding. Tapioca. It's eleven thirty in the morning on a Tuesday, and Jenny's all dressed up—it's still a suit, even if it's slacks—to hand you some papers. Also, we're totally pretending that you didn't conk out at the christening this weekend. Lame."

"Protocol," Jenny corrected.

"And what's that stuff on the speaker, Jenn?"

"Beethoven's Fifth," she answered, as both women knew she would—Jenny was a fiend for classical music.

"You call that lunchtime music?"

"How could you not recognize it?" Alex asked. "It's one of the most famous pieces of music in the world."

"It sucks. Put on some Stones."

"Not even if you threatened to cut off my hands," Jenny said, showing some backbone for a change.

"That's more like it," Christina said approvingly. "Everybody's gotta relax around here. That's all I'm saying."

Alex wanted to say something bitchy yet cutting like "the Alaskan royal family got along fine before you got here" but, of course, that wasn't exactly true. Instead, she held up her empty dessert plate. Instantly, a footman—footwoman, rather—took it from her. What was her name? Something that rhymed with Harry. Mary? Terry? No . . . it was so hard to remember the new ones . . .

"Thank you, Carrie."

"You're welcome, Your Highness. Something else?"

"No, that's fine. Maybe a little more to drink."

She and Chris were enjoying an early lunch; the rest of the family was out and about on various official duties. Alex knew she wouldn't get rid of Christina for a bit; her sister-in-law was deep in Concern Mode.

"Where's Dara?" she asked, changing the subject and smiling a thank-you as her glass of milk was refilled by another footman.

"With her dad in the penguin room. I guess they're keeping an eye on a nest and it's supposed to explode or hatch or whatever any second. It's hard work, getting fish guts out of a toddler's hair."

Alex grinned. "Thankfully your problem, not mine. She slept late this morning."

"Yeah . . ." Christina's hazel eyes were narrow and she was chewing on her lower lip. Her blond hair, recently cut to ear-length, was typically disheveled and she wore her usual outfit of jeans and a white work shirt, no socks, beat-up loafers. Other than the grooms, she was the most casually dressed person on palace grounds "Yeah, that's—I'm not gonna be distracted, by the way. Listen, not that I'm complaining, but don't you think this sort of—of errand or whatever—would be a better job for David?"

Her oldest brother, the Crown Prince, was also Dr. Baranov, with a doctorate in marine biology. Christina was irritating, but right. Which, of course, only made her more irritating. "Yes."

"Well, how come the king didn't ask him to go?"

Alex almost didn't answer. Jenny, who was sitting at the other end of the table to do paperwork (Baranov family protocol was a great deal looser than, say, Windsor family protocol) instantly looked twice as absorbed. Her posture gave off *No, I'm not hearing a word, not a single word, don't give me a thought* vibrations, in the manner of skilled officials the world over.

Alex looked at the top of Jenny's dark head for a long moment, thoughtfully tapped her fruit knife on the edge of the plate, then said, "Because David has a happy, fulfilled, wonderful life and he doesn't want to leave it. Doesn't need to leave it. It was hard enough for him to agree to the Geneva thing, and that's only going to be for three days."

Christina paused in mid-chew, gulped audibly, then forced down the strawberry. "Well, okay." She coughed. "I mean . . . that's okay. Maybe this . . . maybe you'll like it."

"Maybe." Then, "Jenny, will you let Stacy know I'm going to want to talk about wardrobe issues?"

"At once, Highness. And you have a press conference in thirty minutes."

"Very well."

Jenny rose in a graceful rustle of silk and linen, scooped up her paperwork, bowed her head for a moment, and hurried out. She left behind the faintest scent of lilacs.

"Ick," Chris commented, glancing down at her practical clothing. "I'm glad you're going. But I have to say, that's like death to me, the whole thing. Wardrobe meetings, protocol meetings, itinerary meetings, babbling about same to reporters, who actually *write* about it . . ."

Alex smoothed the lapel of her navy blue Travis Avers jacket. Christina's complaints on the subject were nothing new, though they somewhat mystified Alex. Meetings and the press and itineraries were a part of everyday life. Nothing was free . . . not even when your father's picture was on all the money. "That's why you're so cute."

"Don't start, *Princess* Alex."

She laughed. "I won't if you won't, darling plebian sister-in-law."

"Snob."

"Nag."

"Egotist."

"Busybody."

"Stuck up."

"I'll miss our lunches."

"Oh, Alex." Christina's eyes seemed to well for a second and, in an oddly tender moment, she leaned forward and kissed the top of Alex's head. "Sleep."

"Not now, of course. There's too much work to do."

Christina only sighed.

Chapter 5

"**R**ight, right. So, she's going off to Arizona or wherever—"

"North Dakota, Your Majesty." Edmund, standing at attention three feet to the king's left, looked as if he had been born of starch. He was as tall as the king, but much thinner—"have a milkshake for God's sake" thin. His black hair was swept back from his face, which was noble, almost—was it possible?—kingly. Large eyes, strong nose, strong chin . . . many times, Edmund had been mistaken for a member of the royal family. He had been taking care of the Baranovs for decades. "But you were very close."

Christina kept pacing. The reigning king of Alaska, Alexander Baranov II, stayed seated at his desk, working on his word finds. Late afternoon sunlight spilled into the office from the large bay of windows on the left, gifting everything—desk, paperwork, floor, Christina's profile, Edmund's nose—with a golden hue.

"Right, North Dakota. That was my second guess. Well, the winters won't be much of a change for her."

"It's spring, Sir."

"Yeah, whatever," Christina muttered. "So Alex goes

and—what? Everything works out great and she forgives herself?"

King Al looked up and said, almost sharply, "She doesn't have to forgive shit. She did the right thing. She was my brave girl and if she hadn't kicked that guy's ass—"

"Devon's ass, Your Majesty."

"Right, Devon. You'd think I'd be able to remember his name, but it's just one of those things that never stick in my head. Anyway, I would have—"

"Kicked his ass from your coma," Christina sneered, "sure."

"Well, I would have. Watch your mouth, miss. One of the three of us in this room is in charge, and it ain't you."

Edmund cleared his throat modestly.

Christina adopted a more conciliatory tone, an amazing feat no one but the king or her husband could bring about. "Look, I'm not saying she did anything wrong, *you're* not saying she did anything wrong, *Congress* isn't saying she did anything wrong. But obviously she thinks—well, she thinks *something*, or she'd be able to sleep and eat and she wouldn't jump every time somebody picked up a pen. I mean, come on. That's not normal. Freaking out when your brother—your chronically late brother—is late, that's not normal, right?"

"For Princess Alexandria, no. It's not normal."

"I didn't know her for very long before Devon did his little 'time to kill the king and take over the country' shtick, but she just—I mean, *look* at her. You can hardly tell she's pretty."

"An exaggeration, with all respect," Edmund said. "The princess is beautiful every moment."

"Not when she's staggering down the hallway at two thirty in the morning," Christina shot back. "I don't care *how* great-looking she is, nobody looks good at that place and time. And you know why nobody noticed she was gonna faint? Because her normal skin color is 'about to faint' pale."

The king chewed on his thumbnail for a moment. He was an older, male version of Princess Alex, with the trademark Baranov blue eyes, black hair, and quick mind. His fists were the size of bowling balls, dwarfed only by his heart and generosity. "What does Dr. Pohl say about it?" he asked, slowly circling EMBARRASSMENT. "She's gotta have some ideas."

"Oh, she's like a clam. All that patient-client whatever-it-is."

"Privilege, Your Highness."

"Right. Like she said this weekend. Anyway, she's not talking. Not even under extreme nagging. And I bet Alex isn't talking, either. Not to Dr. Pohl, not to us."

"Characteristic," Edmund suggested.

"Annoying," King Al and Christina said in unison.

"So, she'll go. She seems like she wants to go . . . right? Chris, she say anything like she didn't want to go?"

"No, she's already signed off on her outfit lists and all that junk. She's got meetings scheduled and everybody's almost good to go. It's like she came to lunch with her mind made up."

"Well, then." The king circled ASSESSMENT. "Change of scenery, right? Kid might get a kick out of it. Might get some sleep."

"I guess slipping something into her food is totally out of the question."

"Yeah, plus it's against the law to do that to a member of the royal family."

"Also," Edmund prompted, "it's morally wrong and no way to solve a chronic problem."

"Riiiiight," Al and Chris said with convincing sincerity.

"When's she leave? It's on one of my schedules around here . . ." The king gestured to the hundreds of pages in neat piles around his work space. "Along with the grand opening of the new salmon farm."

"The day after tomorrow, Your Majesty."

"Tell her I'd like to have a meeting with her before she takes off. Clear my schedule for tomorrow morning and we'll get it done."

"I'll see to it at once, Sir."

"Al, how many times do we have to talk about this? You don't have meetings with your kid."

"Haven't seen her in a couple of days," the king said absently, circling ABASEMENT. "It's a big place. If I don't catch her now, I gotta catch her later. And I got stuff later."

Christina flung herself into the chair on the other side of the desk and buried her head in her hands. "Don't even start with that."

"Hey, it's meant to be, kiddo."

"Please, Al."

"How can Betty resist this?" he bragged, jerking a thumb at himself. Broad-shouldered, his mane of thick black hair sprinkled with silver, his piercing blue eyes bracketed with laugh lines, the tall, fit monarch had a disturbingly good point. "Read *US* magazine if you don't believe me: I'm a catch, baby."

"Al. Please. I'm begging you."

"What do you care? Don't you have your hands full with Dara and David, not to mention being the Crown Princess? You're probably supposed to be doing something right this minute—"

Edmund coughed. "Signing off on the menu for Easter weekend."

"—but you're in here yakking about Alex. What, you gotta worry about my love life, too?"

"Yes, Al, I have to," she snapped. "We all have to. I think it's safe to say your love life is a global concern."

"Bullshit. Hey, Edmund, where *is* Betty this week, anyway?"

"Her note advises Queen Elizabeth is conducting business in Scotland."

"Bullshit! I just saw her on *CNN* this morning, hanging out at Buckingham for something or other."

"I'm sure Her Majesty the Queen did not deliberately deceive Your Majesty."

"Ha!" Chris said. "Looks like being separated by a continent *and* an ocean isn't enough . . . she's gotta make her secretaries lie to you."

"She will be mine," the king vowed, circling DEPRIVATION.

"You sound like a bad movie villain," the princess snorted. "You've gotta drop the whole 'uniting the houses of Baranov and Windsor' thing. You've just got to. It didn't work five years ago, a year ago, or right now. Don't you think we have enough problems?"

"My courtship is not one of your problems, hon," the king said mildly.

"Says you," she muttered, staring at the ceiling.

"Why don't you make yourself useful? Go gimmee Dara," the king ordered. "I've got some toys for her."

"Al, she's buried in toys. You've got to try to control yourself. The kid's got over 600 teddy bears at last count."

"A few stuffed animals never hurt anyone."

"A few! I tried to find her in her crib the other day and changed a Raggedy Ann doll by mistake."

"Well, honey, you're kind of an idiot."

"Al!"

"It's nothing to be ashamed of, Your Highness."

"Edmund."

"Let's get back on topic," the king said, circling CHAOTIC. "Alex is taking off to find a cure for her insomnia, Dara's the greatest baby in the history of babyhood, her mom's not too bright, and Queen Elizabeth is secretly in love with me."

"I can think of at least three things wrong with that statement," Christina said.

"Only three, Highness?"

"Maybe I should go with her," she said, lapsing into a low mutter no one had ever been able to decipher. "Maybe mmm hmmm bmmm hmmm."

"No," the king said. "She's a big girl. She doesn't need you to come along and bring the nag machine."

"Nobody does, Sir," Edmund coughed.

"Oh, come on, Al. It'll be fun. I can bring Dara! She's never been to America. And you know Alex loves that baby. It's the only way she can sleep sometimes, if she brings the baby to bed with her."

"Forget it, Chris. First off, you have to get my permission *and* Congress's before you take an underage heir out of the country. Second—"

"God *damn* it! She's my kid, too, Al, and she's got dual citizenship."

"Which doesn't cancel the fact that she's an Alaskan citizen, not to mention the heir of the Crown Prince. Kid's probably gonna be queen of Alaska someday, you can't take her to McDonald's without me knowing about it, life sucks, go cry in a bag of money."

"Al, you're killing me! Don't get me started on that *stupid* law—"

"Hey, I don't make the rules."

"You do too!"

"Just saying. Besides, even if you could get your bad self organized in time, it's not a good idea. The baby's a crutch for Alex. I think we can all agree on that."

Since she couldn't argue, Christina remained silent.

"This is something Alex needs to do, alone, we've all agreed on that. And Alex wouldn't be going if *she* didn't agree. Kid's as stubborn as a tick."

"Yet another mysterious recessive gene," Edmund said to the air.

They ignored him. "Anyway. You stay put. Alex goes. And Elizabeth . . . my sweet, sweet Elizabeth . . ."

"Can you grab that letter opener and stab me with it?" Christina begged Edmund. "Make it quick, but be thorough."

"I'm sorry, Your Highness. I need to see to my own end before anyone else's."

"You two are hilarious," the king snapped, circling OBSCENITY. "Don't let the door hit you on the ass on the way out."

Chapter 6

The North Dakota Institute for Sea Life
Minot, North Dakota

". . . it's just such a thrill for us, Your Majesty!"

"Thank you." Alex didn't bother to correct the woman, though only reigning monarchs were referred to as "Majesty." As a lowly princess, Alex would be "Your Highness" unless she became queen which, given the fact that Christina and David were senior to her in the line of succession, was unlikely.

Please, God, let it be unlikely.

Their tour guide had of course been briefed, but people were usually nervous about meeting a member of royalty. Alex herself was nervous about meeting dentists, so she could relate.

And, as an American, Dr. Tiegel didn't have to call her that, or bow . . . which she had also forgotten. But there was no need to correct her, because . . .

"Just a reminder, Dr. Tiegel," Jenny said pleasantly, hurrying to stay abreast of the two women. "Please refer to the princess as Princess Alexandria."

"I'm sorry."

"It's nothing," Alex said with a soothing smile. "It's just a lot of silly protocol, isn't it? There are certainly more important things to worry about, don't you think?"

Instantly at ease, Dr. Tiegel, a plump brunette in her forties, giggled. She was wearing the *de rigueur* white lab coat over a dark pink suit. Her cream-colored blouse sported a bow at the throat the size of Dr. Tiegel's head. Her glossy dark hair was in a Dorothy Hamill bob, further proof that the woman was stuck in the seventies.

"I guess I'm a little nervous. They don't—I mean, I'm from Pierre. South Dakota," she added helpfully. "I've never met a princess before. We're so happy you came to oversee the grand opening."

"It was my great pleasure, and Alaska's." She was trying not to wrinkle her nose, knowing she would soon get used to the smell of fish, penguins, and the offal of sea life. They had all posed for the press outside, but now, in the wee hours, they had the aquarium to themselves. It was a spacious, beautiful building, and the animals Alex could see looked clean, alert, and happy. Many of the exhibits were empty; the NDISL was a work in progress.

"This work is so important, to all of us," she continued. "King Alexander has a special fondness for this sort of thing—he had to pay for the Crown Prince's doctorate in Marine Biology."

Dr. Tiegel giggled again. "We're so glad you could clear your schedule. I guess your brother's busy with his baby?"

"Yes, and he's overseeing the renovation of six aquariums in Alaska." In addition to putting up with Christina, Edmund, their father, helping Christina test the recipes for her cookbook, and teaching Dara her ABCs. Not to mention the Geneva thing nobody could get out of.

Suddenly, Alex was glad to be away. A line from Tolkien popped into her head: "The wide world is all about you; you can fence yourself in, but you cannot for ever fence it out." That sounded like as good a cure for bad dreams as anything.

"We're going to start with the penguin exhibit, if that's all right."

"Of course, as you wish, Dr. Tiegel. And I have to admit, I got a kick out of it when I heard. A land-locked aquarium struck me as unusual."

"Oh, no," Dr. Tiegel said seriously. "There are aquariums in Colorado, Kentucky, Minnesota, Ohio, and Utah, just to name a few. I think you could make a case that they're even more important in places where you wouldn't be able to learn about the oceans on your own."

"I never thought about it like that. Thank you for enlightening me. Shall we start the tour? Where is Doctor . . ." She consulted her itinerary. "Dr. Rivers?"

"Oh, um, Dr. Rivers can't—he isn't—I'm going to do the tour. I mean, I'm honored to do the tour."

Alex raised an eyebrow, but didn't comment. It was unusual for an itinerary to change at the last moment, and she could tell her security team—Reynolds, Danielson, and Krenklov—didn't like it one bit. Jenny was murmuring to Danielson, doubtless telling him there was nothing to worry about. Alex didn't especially care. She had never been remotely concerned about her *own* safety.

"I don't want to put you to any trouble," she said automatically.

"Oh no no no. It's no trouble at all, Princess."

"Is Dr. Rivers ill?" Jenny asked sharply. She would, Alex knew, take any last minute problems as personally as a slap to the head.

"Oh no no no. No. He's fine. He's just—" Alex looked on with interest while Dr. Tiegel stuttered and stammered. Finally, she took pity on the woman.

"I'm looking forward to seeing the rest of the facility."

"Oh, it's a wonderful—you'll love it. Well, we all love it, and we hope you do, too. Okay, well, to begin, as you know, this is the North Dakota Institute for Sea Life. We're a non-profit organization, funded by corporations, private donors, and, of course . . ." Hazel eyes twinkled. ". . . Alaska. If you'll follow me, we'll skirt around the outermost edge of the penguin tank . . ."

Dr. Tiegel opened a small door to the left and led them down a hallway. "These are the labs; most of us work here on various projects as our schedules allow. In fact, some of us sleep here if there's an experiment we don't want to leave."

"Do you do that in addition to taking care of the animals?"

"We really don't need to spend much hands-on time with the animals; most of the feeding and such is handled by volunteers. One of the many purposes of the NDISL is research. For every one thing we know, there are hundreds of thousands of things—more likely millions—we don't know. Of course we have several on-staff biologists and veterinarians to keep an eye on the animals."

"How often do—"

Suddenly, one of the doors was yanked open—Alex had time to notice the stark black lettering (Dr. Sheldon Rivers, Director, Global Marine Programs) before someone (presumably Dr. Rivers) was standing in the doorway.

"Do you have to do this shit here?" he snapped, oblivious to the three guns trained on him. "You've got the whole damn place—twelve thousand square feet!—and you have to have your meeting right outside my door?"

"Shel," Dr. Tiegel began.

"I'm pretty sure I told you about the experiments I can't leave this morning."

"Yes, Shel, but—"

"I mean, I have this memory of standing in your office and explaining why I couldn't play lapdog to her Royal Annoyingness, right?"

Dr. Tiegel winced and Jenny, who had been signaling the security team to put their guns away, suddenly stopped and looked as though she wished she had a gun of her own.

As for Alex, she was having trouble looking away from the furious, infuriating Dr. Rivers. He was so tall and broad he filled the doorway, his cocoa-colored eyes were glaring at them from behind wire-rim frames, his lashes so long they nearly touched the glass. His long legs were showcased in shockingly tattered blue jeans and gaped at the waist; they were about two sizes too large. He was wearing a faded yellow T-shirt with the logo "Marine Biologists Get Wet." No lab coat. His hair, light brown with sun-streaked highlights, stood up from his skull as if he'd been running his fingers through it. His lips were almost too thin, set in a scowl that made his mouth disappear, and his eyes were creased with what might have been laugh lines, but were probably frown lines.

"Now get lost," he said, and shut the door.

On Alex's foot.

Chapter 7

Shel Rivers looked down at the small foot wedged in his doorway, then up at the ridiculously good-looking woman attached to said foot. She didn't look mad or pissed or haughty. Just had a patient look on her face, like "you're gonna get this thing off my foot, right?" Finally, he said, "That's a good way to break something," after a moment that felt longer than it was.

"Not before you get shot," she replied, and shouldered her way past him. A good trick, since he had, at best estimation, four inches and thirty pounds on her. He got a whiff of eucalyptus as she brushed by, and he almost reached out to see if her black, shoulder-length hair was as silky as it looked. "Dr. Rivers and I will be right out," she added, and closed the door on the protests of everyone else in the party.

The princess (princess! in his lab!) looked around the small, cluttered room for a moment, her small hands on shapely hips. Then she glanced back at him. He actually forgot to breathe when those crystal blue eyes fixed on his.

"I don't think we've been properly introduced," she said pleasantly.

"And I don't think your security team is going to like this at all."

"I'm Alexandria Baranov—"

"I know."

"I'm talking now, please. And you're Dr. Rivers. You're also rude and annoying, which is fine, but *nobody* slams a door on me."

"Especially when your family built half the aquarium," he snapped, trying not to look at her breasts.

"Irrelevant. I wouldn't tolerate that behavior if *you* were funding *my* work. What a disaster area," she continued, turning in a circle to take in the whole room. "How do you find anything in here?"

"None of your business."

"I think we could find some paperwork to prove that isn't true. What's so important? What are you working on?"

"Is playing twenty questions part of the tour?"

"No, it's part of being relatively pleasant. And why did you dodge the tour? You don't even know me."

Because she was rich. Because he was busy. Because she was a princess and he was a lowly Army brat. Because she was too beautiful. Because she was trouble with a capital T, and he'd had enough of that to last five lifetimes.

She was waving a hand in front of his eyes. "Dr. Rivers? Helloooooo? Is anyone in there? Is it lunchtime already?"

He jerked his head back and gave her a good glare. "I've got more important things to do than play tour guide for a stuck-up VIP."

He was sure she'd get pissed, but instead, those amazing blue eyes crinkled at the corners and she grinned. "I bet you don't," she said, and turned to reach for the door handle.

"Okay, okay," he said, grasping her elbow. She took his wrist and pulled it away, almost absently, and in the bottom of his brain a small red flag popped up. "I'll give you the damned tour. But no annoying questions."

"You're a fine one to talk about annoying," she retorted.

"And no potty breaks."

"I went on the plane."

"And I'm not going to be doing this all day, either."

"You can't," she pointed out. "I'm having lunch with Dr. Tomlin in three hours."

"Another rich fat cat," he muttered.

"Did you just call me fat?"

"Hardly. In fact, when was the last time you had a meal?" She was gorgeous—she more than lived up to her moniker as one of the most beautiful women in the world—but too skinny. The planes in her face made her blue eyes seem enormous. "Or even a milkshake?"

"I don't know," she said absently. "It's probably on the schedule somewhere."

Another red flag popped, and he was so intrigued he almost forgot about his experiments. "Well, there's a snack bar on the second floor. Maybe we can grab some fries or something. Although, once you have to watch Dr. Tomlin eat, you're gonna lose your appetite. Assuming you ever had one."

"That's all right, Dr. Rivers."

"Shel."

"Shel. You don't have to worry. I'm not even hungry. And I'm Alex, by the way."

He shook her small, cool hand. His wrist was almost twice the width of hers. Definitely needed a few milkshakes, among other things.

"It's nice to meet you, Alex."

"What a lie, Dr. Rivers."

He smiled in spite of himself.

Chapter 8

The Sitka Palace
Juneau, Alaska

"**S**o, how's she doing?" the king asked, glancing up from the bill he was reading.

Edmund handed him two reams of paperwork. "Fine, Your Majesty. They landed without incident; she's at the facility right now."

"When's she due back?"

"Nineteen days, Sire."

"Nineteen days? How long's it take to look at a bunch of fish?"

"Your Majesty—"

"I mean, I know we talked about her meeting up with all the funders and—and whatever the hell else she's doing out there, but nineteen friggin' days?"

"She'll be fine, Sire."

The king glowered, blue eyes—eyes he'd passed on to all his children—narrowing. "I'm pretty sure I didn't agree to the kid disappearing into the wilds of North Dakota for almost three weeks. I agreed to a quick trip. I agreed things couldn't go on the way they were. I agreed the shrink wasn't helping. I did not agree to the kid disappearing for practically a damn month."

"Sire, you agreed she was ready for a change."

"I smell you and Jenny all over this one, buddy boy, don't think I don't."

"Yes, Sire."

"I would have remembered a nineteen-day itinerary. I'm not that fucking senile."

"Don't underestimate yourself, Sire."

"Knock it off, Edmund. A quick trip to this aquarium place, *that's* what we talked about."

"Yes, Sire."

"The kid's only twenty-three, she's never been away from home for more than—than—what?"

"Fifteen days. And Her Highness is twenty-five."

"Oh, sure, throw that in my face, you scheming son of a bitch."

"Sire, it was bad enough when you arranged for the professors to come to the palace so she could earn her degree without ever moving out. Nineteen days, at her age, is nothing. She'll be fine, Sire."

The king drummed his blunt fingers on the desk. "It's just that she's had a tough year."

"Yes, Sire."

"You know, she's not sleeping, she's not eating—we gotta keep an eye on her."

"Yes, Sire."

"I know she looks tough, but she's fragile."

"Like a precious baby duck, Sire."

The king's frown deepened. "What are you up to, Edmund?"

"Not a tiny thing, Sire."

"Just because you're six times smarter than me doesn't mean I can't kick your ass."

"I'm well aware, Sire."

"Okay, I won't jump a plane to bring her back—"

"You can't, Sire, you have a meeting with the Tourism Commission in thirty minutes."

"—but I want updates on what she's doing at least twice a day."

"Creepy, Sire."

"Oh, you know what I mean. Just keep me informed. You know, pretend like I'm your boss or something and you have to do what I say or you're breaking the law."

"Jenny will keep us updated, Sire, and Her Highness will do as she pleases."

"My ass!"

"Have you met Princess Alexandria, Sire?"

"She'll do what she's told. I'm her king and I'll do you one better than that . . ." He jabbed a thumb the size of a small banana at his chest. "I'm her *father*."

"I'm sure she will tremble and obey, Sire."

"My ass," he said again, quietly.

"I dream of the day we can have a meeting without talking about your ass. As to the other, most likely the princess's independence is a recessive gene of some kind, sure to be stamped out in future generations."

"Aw, shutcher face. And I mean it about keeping me up to date."

"It will be as you command, my king."

"That'd be the fucking day."

Chapter 9

North Dakota Institute for Sea Life
Minot, North Dakota

". . . and that's pretty much it."

"Fascinating," Alex commented.

"Yeah?"

She smiled. "My brother isn't the only one interested in marine biology. He was just the only one who wanted to go to school for years and years to learn about it. I thought my father was going to have a nervous breakdown." At Shel's quizzical look, she elaborated. "It was very hard on him when David went away to school."

"Oh."

"You know. Parents."

"Yeah. You know, I read about your bro somewhere," he said, almost reluctantly. "Got his Bachelor's in three years, his Master's in a year and a half, and his PhD in two years."

"Yes," she said cheerfully. "He's a tremendous geek. Definitely the brains in the family."

"I dunno," he said, giving her a sideways glance. "Your knuckles don't exactly drag on the floor when you walk. Congratulations. You got through the tour without a single stupid question."

She smiled graciously. "So did you."

Shel laughed, and she had to look away. He had a great laugh and it took years off his face. She was trying to figure out if she was attracted to him because of his handsome face, killer long legs, or because he'd been so rude. Nobody was ever rude to her. It made for a refreshing change of pace.

"I appreciate your time, Dr. Rivers."

"Shel. And it was no trouble, Princess."

"Alex. And aren't you afraid you'll go to Hell for lying?" she teased.

"Hardly. I've lived in Guam; I've already been in Hell."

"What were you doing there?"

"Army brat," he replied shortly. "My dad was posted."

"My dad was in the military, too—"

"I'll bet! Wasn't he, like, King-General-in-Chief?"

"Hardly," she said primly. "And such nasty assumptions you make, Dr. Rivers. In my country, military service isn't mandated for the royal family. My father joined because he wanted to. Also, his mother was driving him crazy. But we were talking about your homes. I've never lived anywhere but Alaska. Have you been?"

"Yeah. Also Germany, France, Iceland, Great Britain, Gitmo, Italy, and Kentucky."

She found that quite fascinating, though from the tone of his voice it wasn't a topic up for much further discussion. "How interesting. This is my first time in North Dakota."

"Yeah, I figured. I mean, who's gonna come here if they don't have to?"

"You don't like it here?"

"Actually, I kind of love it here."

"It's very beautiful. Different from home, but still lovely. You can *see*, here. For miles and miles. At home, the trees crowd right up to the road. It can be a little claustrophobic, especially if you're used to . . ." She held out an arm, indicating the state of North Dakota. "This."

He was silent for a long moment, and when he spoke, it sounded like he was strangling. "It's my place. I picked it. Nobody dragged me here and then dragged me away. Nobody stuck me somewhere and waited until I made friends and then stuck me somewhere else. North Dakota's mine."

She nodded.

"It's the only thing that's ever been mine."

"Yes, Dr. Rivers."

"I guess you wouldn't know about that."

"I know about being stuck."

He snorted. "Sure you do."

"It's not an exclusive province of the children of Army officers."

"Or royalty."

She looked at him. "Oh. I see. You're one of those assholes who assume that the rich don't have problems."

"I don't think princesses are allowed to use the word 'assholes.'"

"Trust me, Dr. Rivers, you wouldn't know a damn thing about it."

"Oh, come on! Like someone who has never once had to worry about buying food or paying the electric bill really has problems?"

"Good-bye, Dr. Rivers," she said, and abruptly strode away, waving to Jenny who was waiting for her at the end of the corridor.

"Shel!" he yelled after her.

Chapter 10

"Hi."

"Hi."

"So."

"Yeah."

"How've you been?"

"Fine. You?"

"Oh, you know. The usual things. Not much has happened in the four hours since I last saw you."

"Well, kind of a lot has happened on my end," Shel explained.

"Yes, I see that," Alex replied.

"Thanks for coming."

"Well, I felt it was the least I could do."

"No, you didn't have to."

"It's all right," she said kindly. "I felt we had some unfinished business."

"I kind of felt that way, too. I mean, that's the whole reason I'm here."

"I understand."

Alex could hear the click of heels, and didn't have to turn

away from the bars to know Jenny had entered the small room.

"Oh, dear," she said, staring at Shel. Her small nose wrinkled, and Alex knew why; she'd seen her fair share of jail cells. They all smelled like laundry soap, sweat, and piss. "Oh, oh dear."

"Hi," he said, waving at her from his side of the cell.

Jenny ran a distracted hand through her newly shorn brunette bob. "Oh, Dr. Rivers. Oh, oh, oh."

"Don't tell me you've never had to bail out one of your little chickadees before."

"She hasn't," Alex informed him. "But we've visited friends on occasion."

"Royal pals in the clink!" Shel said gleefully. "Film at eleven!"

"What is Dr. Tiegel going to say? What will the press say?" Jenny cried.

"What will my father say?" Alex suggested, because she had a vicious streak and wanted to see Jenny go even paler, if possible.

"Your father. Your father!" Jenny started walking in small, distracted circles. "I will, of course, be blamed for this, and he's right to blame me, I should have guessed you'd try something idiotic and ridiculous."

"Hey!" Shel protested. "I just wanted to see your boss again, that's all. We sort of left on the wrong foot."

"Actually, the wrong foot was wedged into your big fat mouth," Alex said helpfully.

"So I thought it'd be cool to sneak in and see you and apologize."

"Only to be tackled, cuffed, and hauled away by my ever-vigilant security team, then tossed in jail."

"Look, in the movies it would have worked. It would have been romantic and cool." He managed to get the sullen look off his face for half a second. "Thanks again for coming down."

"How could I stay away, once I was told what you'd been up to?" she teased.

Jenny was shaking her head. "Dr. Rivers, what world do you live in?"

"An adorable one," Alex said, and linked fingers with him through the bars. "You idiot."

"Aw." He blushed.

"Stop that!" Jenny snapped. "We have to focus on the PR aspects of this boneheaded stunt, not how cute he looked in his mug shot."

"So you admit I'm cute!" he said triumphantly.

"No," a new voice said. "You're as ugly as the south end of a north-bound skunk."

Shel waved at the man, a striking green-eyed blond whose shoulder-length hair was pulled back in a ponytail.

"Oh," Jenny said. She actually dropped her clipboard, which hit the cement floor with a clatter. After a long moment, Alex bent and picked it up.

"This is my best friend," Shel was gesturing through the bars, "Teal Grange."

"Oh," Jenny said.

Alex wrapped Jenny's fingers around the clipboard.

"Teal, this is the Princess of Alaska—"

"I know who she is, pal. We get *People* magazine in Minot."

"—and her majordomo assistant-type gal, Jenny—uh, I can't remember your last name."

"It doesn't matter," Jenny said, clearly dazzled. Teal was only a few inches taller than she was, but powerfully built . . . his navy tee-shirt bulged in interesting places, and he had the powerful look of a regular lifter. The fluorescent lights bounced off his glasses and made his moss-green eyes unreadable. The scowl, however, spoke volumes.

"Hi." Teal shook hands with Jenny, who forgot to put hers away. It hung in the air, a small white bird without a nest. "Hi, Princess."

"Hello." They would certainly, she thought, make a beautiful couple; Jenny's willowy dark beauty and his blunt blond All-American good looks. "It's nice to meet you."

"Me, too!" Jenny blurted, then blushed to her hairline when they all looked at her. "I mean, it's nice to meet you, too. That's all I meant to say."

"I've come to bail out Dr. Dumbass."

"That's so cute," Alex said. "My sister-in-law makes up annoying names for her friends, too. It was nice of you to—"

"He's my one phone call," Shel admitted.

"But it's not necessary."

"Oh, one of your guards is gonna shoot him? That's good; it'll save time. Plus, I can get back to the *CSI* marathon."

Alex laughed, but Jenny never cracked a smile; she was staring raptly into Teal's gorgeous green eyes. "There's no—there's no need to bail anyone out, Mr. Grange."

"Teal. Mr. Grange is my brother."

"Yes, of course. Your brother. Yes. Ah . . . the Baranov family acknowledges this was an unfortunate misunderstanding, and of course Dr. Rivers will be free to go as soon as we finish some rudimentary paperwork. It won't take long at all, you have my word . . . Teal."

Nice, Alex thought, amused. *What if he'd had a gun? Or a rope? Jenny's got a crush, so my security goes out the window. I'm dead of strangulation, but she gets laid.*

"Hey," Shel said. Then, louder: "Hey! That's really nice of you, Jenny."

"You're welcome," she replied, not looking at Shel. "How—how do you know Dr. Rivers?"

"Are we still in the room?" Shel muttered to her.

Alex shook her head.

Teal's scowl disappeared into a grin. "Oh, I went to high school with the dumbass here, me and my brother."

"Spent one year with him, then I couldn't shake any of them for the rest of my life," Shel volunteered.

"Hey, am I down here at ten o'clock at night to bail your sorry ass out? Yeah. Are you the most ungrateful dumbass on the planet?"

"Yes," Jenny said, dazzled. Then, "Any of them? You couldn't shake any of them?"

"I'm over here," Shel called helpfully. "In the cell."

"Shut up, Dr. Dumbass," Teal commanded. "The lady's obviously talking to me."

Alex snickered, and Shel continued. "Teal's got a bunch of sibs. Tell her. She looks like she could use a good laugh."

"Crane, Robin, Crow, and Raven."

"No way," Alex said, blinking.

"Bunch of bird-brained morons, each one of them," Shel muttered.

"My parents," Teal explained with exaggerated patience, "were ornithologists."

"How interesting! That's so interesting. I'm really interested in hearing more about your—er—interesting family."

Teal smiled at her and Alex could see the attraction; she could actually feel the man's smile in her knees. Blondes weren't really her type, but . . . poor Jenny!

"Anybody ever tell you that you look like Shania Twain?"

"Uh-huh," she replied.

"Date later!" Shel shouted, startling everybody. "Bail first!"

"I think I can take care of that," Alex said, which was just as well, because Jenny wasn't listening anymore.

Chapter 11

"Thanks for walking me to—er—where are we going, anyway?"

"I worked on the polar bear exhibit after you took off. I thought you'd like to see it."

"Oh, your bear came in?"

Shel shook his head. He was getting a headache from trying to look at her out of the corner of his eye. Even while walking down a muddy sidewalk in beat-up sneakers (were princesses allowed sneakers?), she was breathtaking. He couldn't believe she was out with him, here, now. Hell, he couldn't believe she'd come downtown to grease the skids so he didn't have to spend the night in a cell!

Then, cool as a cuke, she tells Jenny and the guards (nice enough fellows with hands like iron), "That will be all for tonight," and like that, he was walking her out and they were climbing into her car. No press—it was late, and Jenny had probably gotten rid of them.

The car pulled up to the back entrance of the NDISL, and they both got out. "That will be all for tonight, Kara," she told her driver. "I'll make other arrangements to return to the hotel."

"Highness," Kara replied, touching her cap with a forefinger, and pulled smoothly away from the curb.

"Is that smart?" he asked, watching the red taillights grow smaller in the distance. "What if someone tries to kidnap you or whatever?"

"Someone like who?" She gestured to the deathly quiet streets of Minot.

"Well, you know. Someone. There could be an elaborate plot to snatch you. I mean, it was in the papers. You coming here."

She shrugged. "You'll have to protect me, I guess."

"I could be in on it. I could be the mastermind!"

Another shrug. The woman, he mused, either truly didn't give a rat's butt for her own safety, or possessed the acting ability to make it appear that way.

"Aren't you worried about your own safety? I mean, you're a public figure worth big bucks."

"No."

"No, you're not worth big bucks?" he teased, because even in the near-dark, he could see she was stiffening up.

"No, I don't care. Shall we go? You said your bear was here?"

"No, I never had a chance to answer. The big guy's showing up tomorrow. I thought I'd show you his habitat."

"Almost as fascinating a sight," she said, "as the city jail."

"Yeah, yeah."

". . . and in a year or so, we're hoping to get him a mate."

"How enthralling."

"You don't have to be a jerk about it," he said, trying not to be hurt. Then mad at himself because he was trying . . . or even hurt! "If it's not interesting to you, just say so. I can take it."

"No, it's interesting," she said, poking a toe at one of the piles of snow.

The habitat was large—bigger, Shel thought, than his own apartment—and cool, with piles of snow everywhere, and a large pool off to the left. Since it was currently bear-free, the place had a fresh, clean smell.

"He'll get a lady friend in here, will he?"

"Yes."

"Hmm."

She was walking around with her hands clasped behind her back, just like a dignitary. A dignitary in spotless jeans, a spotless white blouse, and sneakers. Her black hair looked like a starless night against the starkness of her shirt and the cool white of the habitat. Her lips were pursed in thought, but it was too close to looking like she was ready for a kiss, and he had to look away.

"So, you're hoping to get cubs out of the deal?"

"Ideally."

"Assuming she accepts the fellow you picked out for her."

"Well . . ." He could feel the blood filling his face and told himself to grow the hell up. He was a scientist, for Christ's sake, not a giggling high school freshman. "Polar bears are solitary, actually. So we'll only put them together for mating purposes. She'll have her own habitat most of the time. And they'll—if they're compatible, they'll mate several times in one week."

"So, they'll do it again and again and again, and then she'll go back to her own place?"

He coughed. "Yeah."

"Now that *is* enthralling," she said, and pounced on him like a big cat. He was so startled he staggered back, clutching at her, and they toppled into one of the snow banks.

Her lush mouth clamped over his, and her arms curved

around his neck. He clawed for air and gasped, "You must really be into polar bears."

"Dr. Rivers," she murmured, fumbling with his belt buckle, "shut the hell up."

He did, and tried not to gasp again when her chilly hands closed over his dick. Cool or not, he was *very* happy to see her. He fumbled for the buttons on her blouse and got them open with fingers that felt like flippers. Her breasts, pale white with rose-colored nipples, filled his hands. Her scent filled his nose; his face was hidden in the dark blaze of her hair.

They wriggled against each other, working out of their jeans, and then her knees were on either side of his hips and he was thrusting up into her. She was tight, and dry, and, if possible, more determined than he was.

"Wait—"

"No."

"I can—"

"It's fine," she gasped.

The last of the blood left his brain and cognitive thought became a thing of the past. Before he could do just about any crossword in pen, now his thoughts were reduced to: Yum smell. Feel good. Want more. Sleepy soon.

He had to have been hurting her—hell, the friction was almost hurting *him*—but she didn't seem to mind, seemed to be enjoying it. She'd thrown her head back and was rocking against him, bracing her palms behind her on his thighs. He groaned as his climax didn't so much approach as gallop up to him, overtake him, bury him.

"Oh my *God*," he managed, as she stopped rocking, as she surged forward to look down at him and her hair swung into her face. "You're an angel!"

She grinned. "Keep it between us, please. I don't think the *Minot Daily News* needs to know about my angelic properties."

"This snow bank is freezing," he complained. It was actually the first time he'd really noticed, but snow had gone down his collar and up his ass.

"What a whiner," she said good-naturedly, and climbed off him. In seconds, she had arranged her clothing and was standing patiently, waiting for him to get his act together.

"Well!" he said brightly, brushing snow off his jeans. "That was . . . that was really nice. I'm sorry you didn't—"

She waved a hand at him. "I had fun. It was fine."

"Yeah, but I think I had I *more* fun, physiologically speaking, if you know what I—"

"It's fine, I said."

What was going on here? He frowned at her but she seemed not to notice. She was more distant and chilly than usual, acting like—well, acting almost like a guy who'd gotten his and now wanted to be gone.

"I'll—I'll give you a ride back to the hotel," he said.

"That would be great."

"Maybe you want to get a drink or something first?"

"No," she replied. "I'm really tired."

"Yeah, I guess you've got another big day tomorrow."

"I guess you're right."

Well, fine. We both got ours and now we're being adults about it.

Then how come he felt so shitty?

Chapter 12

"This has been nice," she said as they pulled up to the hotel.

"Yeah, a laugh a minute," he said flatly. He put the car in park and slung an arm over the back of the seat, looking at her. "That's a new one for me. The snow bank."

She giggled; she couldn't help it. "Not for me. I'm from Alaska."

At last, at last he smiled. Oh, she loved that smile. "Spare me your snowy lovemaking ways. On second thought, don't."

There was a pause, and she realized he was waiting for her to invite him up to her room.

"Thanks again for—" The tour. The smile. The fabulous big cock. The laugh. The ride. The other ride. "—for everything."

"No big. Are you sure you don't . . . uh . . . need anything?"

"No. It's been a long day, and Jenny's going to want to debrief me. I'd better get up there."

"Yeah, okay. Well, see you later."

"I'm not sure," she replied, "I'll have to check my schedule." She opened her car door and stuck a leg out, only to stop in surprise when she felt his arm on her elbow.

"Just a minute here," he said, squinting at her in the sudden glare of the dome light. "Just so we're clear, *I'm* giving *you* the brush-off. Right? I mean, we had a one-night stand and now I'm the one saying that was nice, see you never."

"Oh, of course," she assured him. "That seems fine to me."

"Wait a minute!"

She stopped again in mid climb. "What?"

"It sounds like you think *you're* the one giving *me* the brush-off."

"Well, I'm really going to be very busy in the next few weeks . . ."

"So am I!"

"Okay," she said, trying to keep her temper. What the hell was this guy getting so worked up over? Not to sound like a reverse chauvinist, but he was a guy. He got laid and there weren't any strings. He should be zooming off into the dark, singing a happy tune. "So I guess this is good-bye."

"Like hell it is!" he nearly shrieked.

"For God's sake, will you keep it down? There *are* people with guns around, you know."

"I've got news for you, *Princess*. We're going on a *date*. Tomorrow."

"But my itinerary . . ."

"Shove your itinerary up your tight ass."

"You never mind my ass!" she cried, stung.

"We're going out. This was *not* a one-night stand. Repeat," he added through gritted teeth, "after me."

"This was *not* a one-night stand," she parroted obediently.

"Damn right it wasn't! So cancel whatever you have to cancel; I'm picking you up at seven."

"We could have a nice dinner in my hotel room," she suggested.

"You're damn right we could!"

She finally escaped from the car, and watched from the sidewalk as he roared off.

Chapter 13

The phone was ringing as she stepped into her hotel suite. Jenny rose to meet her, picked up the phone, and said, "Good evening, Your Majesty . . . yes, she's right here . . . at once, Sir."

Alex took the phone, covered the receiver with her palm, and whispered, "I have to shift some things around tomorrow night."

Jenny looked vaguely alarmed. "Yes, Princess."

"I'll tell you about it later. Get to your own room; it's late."

"Yes, Princess, and good night."

Alex slumped onto the couch, returned Jenny's wave, kicked off her shoes, and said, "What are you still doing up, Dad?"

"Me? How about you? It's, what, three o'clock in the morning there? The hell? What have you been doing?"

"Meeting the locals." She swallowed a yawn. "Shouldn't you be signing a bill into a law or something?"

"Off my case, you little jerk. Did you know about this?"

"About what, Dad?" she asked patiently.

"That this little trip was going to be practically for a month!"

"Dad, my schedule's been on your desk for over a week."

"So? I still say they tricked me."

"Read your damn schedules," she told the king, "and quitcher bitchin'."

"Nice way to talk to your father. And your sovereign!"

"I beg your pardon, Your Majesty."

He chuckled. "Bet *that* tasted bad."

"I can do the dance when I want. We all can, isn't that right? How's the baby?"

"Fiendishly smart."

"How's Nicky?"

"Got tossed out of A.L. Prep for blowing up the teacher's lounge."

"Ooooh, ouch! What a budding sociopath you're raising, Your Majesty."

"Me! This is all Edmund's fault. I just have to figure out how. The boy's on his way back; he's due in here a couple hours. Then he gets the reaming of his life. You're lucky you're there, because the press is going apeshit here."

She shuddered. "Makes me glad I'm a thousand miles away. On the other hand, if people think he's dangerous, they won't mess with him."

"Uh . . . yeah." The king coughed. "Anybody giving you trouble out there? Funds doing okay?"

"Dad, it's only been a day, my funds are fine. And everybody's very nice. Except this one guy—Dr. Rivers."

"So, get rid of him."

"No, I kind of like that he's so grumpy. Seriously, I don't think he gives a tin shit that I'm a Baranov."

"I smell fortune hunter."

"You wouldn't if you'd seen his . . . clothes." She'd almost said "underwear."

"They're the worst kinds. The poor ones."

"I thought you said the ones who had a little money but were greedy for more were the worst ones."

"Well, they're more guidelines than rules. I still think you should get rid of him if he's bugging you. Have Jenny take care of it."

"I dunno, he's okay." She could hear herself slipping into her father's speech pattern; the first voice she had ever heard, the one she loved the most. "I'm thinkin' about seein' him again tomorrow."

"Oh."

"Like I said, he's bugging me, but in a good way."

"Seeing him, like on a date?"

"That's what he said. Insisted, actually."

"Well, good for you! And you may, once I get the paperwork on him—"

"Dad!"

"—and Jenny and your guards turn in their reports—"

"Daaaaaaaaaaad!"

"What? It's standard op, sweetie."

"Embarrassing, is what it is," she grumbled.

"Tough titty."

"Language!"

"Look who's talking," he said, and laughed and hung up with a loud click.

Chapter 14

"... and we've moved the fund-raising dinner to Wednesday, to accommodate your ... private meeting ... with Dr. Rivers."

"Snarky, snarky," Alex said, not looking up from the newspaper.

"He isn't worthy of your interest, Your Highness, and I can't help it if that's how I feel." Jenny's lip actually curled. Alex was amazed. "Dr. Rivers. Hmph."

"You sound about sixty years old when you do that."

"He could have shown more respect."

"Yes, he could have," she said, smiling. "But he didn't."

Her suite was on the eastern side of the hotel, and the sun had come up in a blaze of spring glory, making all the silverware and dishes look as though they were on fire. Truly, a gorgeous day. And best of all, no nightmares! Instead, she had paced and thought and fretted and read, the grumpy Dr. Rivers never far from her mind.

"Another thing, Your Highness, if you'll allow me."

"Mmmm?"

"I don't think—that is—I noticed that—"

She yawned. "Spit it out, Jenn."

"I don't think forcing yourself to stay awake is the best solution for your . . . problem."

Alex turned the page, skimmed the "Lifetime" section, read about her arrival in town, and after the long, heavy silence, Jenny took the hint and busied herself with returning phone calls and distributing the many flower bouquets sent to honor the Princess on her journey to the Midwest.

"**O**oooh," Teal teased, walking into Shel's office. "Got a big date?"

"As a matter of fact, yes." He was practically strangling himself trying to get the knot right in his tie, and for what? *She* certainly didn't seem the type to care. "And you're coming with me."

"Aw." Teal moved a stack of journals to one side and sat in the chair. "That's really sweet, Shel, but I think of you as a friend. I'm not saying I don't find you attractive, because you're a good-looking guy, but I think we shouldn't risk ruining our friendship by taking it to the next level."

"Are you done?"

"No. Be gentle, it's my—"

"Shut the hell up and help me tie this thing." Teal obligingly got up and, with a few deft motions, had a neat Windsor tied. Shel nearly cried with relief. "Thanks."

"I can tie a fly on a line so fine you can't see it, I can do a tie. Anything for you, beautiful."

"And you're coming with me, like I said. I'm seeing Alex, and you're going to take her 'I must be everywhere the Princess is' gal-pal out."

Teal's green eyes widened. "Jenny? That gorgeous brunette who looks like—"

"Shania Twain, yeah, yeah, I heard you babbling about that while I was rotting in jail. That American singer, right?"

"Canadian, you dumbass. And ninety minutes of cell time isn't exactly rotting—"

"So will you do it?"

"No."

"Goddammit!"

Teal sighed and looked down at his red T-shirt and faded jeans. "Not that I wouldn't love some face time with the looker, but I'm not really dressed for it."

"Good. They won't suspect we're trying to break them up."

"Oh, brain–dead, are they?"

"Just shut up and get your coat."

"You're so bitchy when you're trying to get laid."

"Coat. Grab. Now."

"I notice you didn't deny it."

"Move faster."

"Has the Princess seen this side of you?"

"Sure."

"Just checking."

Chapter 15

"They're on the way up," Jenny reported.

" 'They'?"

"Apparently Dr. Rivers felt the need for a chaperone." This in a tone of grudging approval.

Alex raised her eyebrows. "You're kidding."

"No, Highness."

"A chaperone?"

"Yes, Highness."

"Weird."

"No, proper."

"Proper!" the princess hooted. "Ha! Exactly the sort of thing that springs to mind when I think of Shel Rivers."

There was a quick rap at the door. It was pushed open by one of her team members, and in walked Shel and his nice-looking friend, the fellow with the funny name.

"Hello, Mr. Grange!" Jenny said, with a little more enthusiasm than Alex privately thought was necessary.

"Teal," he corrected her, holding out a ham-size hand for her to shake. "Nice to see you again."

Jenny flicked invisible dust off her lapels. "It was kind of you to accompany Dr. Rivers this evening."

"Yes," Grange replied, pushing his glasses further up on his nose. "It sure as shit was."

"I'm afraid I only had dinner sent up for two," Jenny said nervously, smoothing her navy skirt. Alex wondered if she'd start disrobing out of sheer nervousness. Had she ever seen Jenny this jittery? She had not. "But I can certainly call and—"

"Why don't we go out?" Teal asked.

"Oh. Oh! I, uh, couldn't do that." She gestured in Alex's direction. "My job. I mean, the princess. I mean, I can't do that. But you're very very very very very very nice to ask. Really nice." She gasped for breath. "Very very nice."

"Are you all right?" Dr. Rivers asked, honestly puzzled.

"Yes," she said, fanning herself with sheet six of the day's itinerary.

Alex pinched her lower lip between her thumb and forefinger, so she wouldn't laugh. She'd never seen Jenny look so defiant and crushed (and cyanotic!) at the same time. "Don't be silly," she said, after she was sure she wouldn't snort, or giggle. "You and Teal can go out. Dr. Rivers and I can stay here in my suite."

"Your Highness—"

"Security's a lot better here than at the—than at other places," Shel pointed out cheerfully. He winked at her and, feeling like a conspirator, Alex winked back.

"No no no no no, I couldn't."

"Sure you could," Teal said, grabbing her by the elbow. "You like Chinese? No? Good, because the closest Chinese place sucks. How about American? You like American? I know a great burger place. They serve 'em as big as your head!"

"But—"

"Bye," Alex said, holding the door for them.

"But—"

"Bye," Shel said, closing the door on them.

They looked each other in the sudden silence of the room, and burst out laughing.

Chapter 16

"First trip to Minot?"

"Yes," Jenny replied stiffly.

"So, whaddya think?"

"It's very nice."

"Are you, uh, gonna be this tense all night?"

"I shouldn't be here," she explained. "My job."

"Like that Alex gal would let you hang around if she didn't want you to."

"Well," Jenny began helplessly.

"Besides, I jumped at the chance to see you again."

Jenny nearly knocked over her water glass. "You—you did?"

"Sure." He sucked up a terrifying mound of spaghetti, then downed the rest of his beer, then took another bite. "Your burger okay?" he asked with his mouth full.

"It's fine, I had actually eaten before you arrived."

"Well, shit, why'd you order it?"

"You ordered it," she reminded him. "But it's fine. As I said, it was kind of you to take me out."

"You kiddin'? I haven't been able to quit thinking about you, good lookin'. Has anyone ever told you—"

"Yes." She couldn't help smiling a little. "Including you."

"Well, there you go. Not that there's not more to you than being really pretty."

"Oh, there isn't," Jenny replied straight-faced.

"Finally, she loosens up!"

"You're very—I mean, I like your outfit."

"Aw, come off it. I said I jumped at the chance to see you again; I didn't say I had any advance warning. You think I dress like *this* for a date?"

"I'm not dressed well, either," she admitted.

"What, you kidding? You look like a million bucks."

"This is a second-day suit," she explained. "Something I wear on the job. Not at all appropriate for private socializing."

"Well. I didn't want to say anything, but you *do* look a little . . . starchy."

"Oh, that's good," she said earnestly.

"You should get yourself some jeans and a few T-shirts. Maybe some a' those, what do you call them . . . the rubber sandals—flip flops!" he finished triumphantly as the words came. "Red ones."

"Oh, no."

"Oh, yes." He leered at her in a friendly way and beckoned to the waitress. "So, how long do you think those two are going to need to do it?"

This time she did knock over her water glass, then sat in embarrassed silence until the waitress cleaned up the mess and departed. "I—uh—that's really none of my—our—concern."

"God, you act like you never had to do a discreet vamoose while the princess got some mmm-hmm." He raised a fist to eyebrow level and wiggled it back and forth.

"It's not part of my job description," she replied stiffly.

"I bet you could write a book filled with all the shit you do that isn't in your job description."

"I would *never*."

"Okay, okay, calm down, I don't have a book contract in my pocket. Listen, I figure, two hours should do it. I mean, I've got to get up early tomorrow for work. And I bet you do, too. And frankly, Shel can't be *that* good."

"What—what is it you do?"

"I'm a hunting and fishing guide."

"Oh, how interesting."

"Yeah? Because you sounded less than thrilled."

"I'm so sorry. I didn't mean to. It's just . . . I'm from Alaska. Hunting and fishing is a primary way of life for most people."

"Oh, yeah? So it's like a guy telling you he sells copiers or whatever?"

She smiled. "Something like that."

"So, what's your dream date's dream job?"

"We shouldn't be talking about this. Your job is fine. Honorable. It's fine. It's really fine."

"Come on . . . fess up. What's your future husband's dream job?"

"That's private," she said primly.

"Stripper? Candygram guy? Cop? Palace guard?"

"It's none of your business, Mr. Grange."

He beat the table with the palms of his hands. "Come onnnnnnnnnnnnnnnnnn."

"Mr. Grange."

He pouted, which was alarming on a man as large as he was. "Fine, don't tell me."

"As should be clear, I wasn't planning to."

"Exotic dancer? Cab driver? Kindergarten teacher? Paramedic?"

"I must admit, the more you snivel, the less I want to tell you."

"Oh yeah? Well, I'm all done sniveling, how about that?"

She stifled a sigh as she stole another glance. It was

ridiculous, how wonderful he looked, even in casual clothes. Normally she liked her men in Saville Row, but Teal looked fabulous despite what he was wearing. It was the broad shoulders, she decided. No, the hair. No, the glasses—they made him look smart and tough. No, the eyes. The green, green eyes. A pity he was so childish. So large and childish. And large.

And perhaps the smallest bit insensitive. Imagine, she had mentioned her vegetarian proclivities in the car and he had *still* ordered her a burger.

"—should be safe to go back after dessert."

"Of course," she replied.

"You want to split a tiramisu?"

"Of course," she said again.

The eyes. Definitely the eyes.

Chapter 17

Shel stared at Alex, then stared at her some more. Curled up like a cat on the cream-colored chaise lounge, she looked back and raised her dark brows.

"Penny," she said after a long moment.

"Honestly? I was thinking that you're the most gorgeous woman I've ever seen."

"Ever?" she teased. "Ever ever? Or ever in real life ever? Because I think Halle Berry is much prettier."

"Ever ever. Women on their wedding days don't look as good as you look in—what are those, little pants?"

"Clam diggers," she said, giggling into her palm. "Little pants? Did you think they'd shrunk in the wash?"

"I don't know," he said impatiently. "Come here."

She got up from her seat and bent over him. Her black hair fell into his face as they kissed, and her perfume was like spring, and her mouth was like silk.

"Oh, boy," she said against his mouth.

"Right," he said, pulling at her, fumbling at her. "Is there a bed in this place?"

"Somewhere around here. Don't tug, Jenny didn't let me pack very many T-shirts."

"Oh, fuck that. We'll hit a souvenir shop later, you can load up."

"No," she said, and laughed. "Fuck me."

"Oh, boy." This time he said it.

Alex yawned. "Mm-hmm, that was an energetic twenty minutes."

"Twenty-five," he corrected. *Energetic twenty minutes.* Jesus Christ, she was just like a guy. Weren't women supposed to be all google-eyed and mushy about sex? Especially just afterward? Shouldn't she be halfway in love with him by now? Why wasn't she, dammit? Why wasn't she all soft-eyed and sexily smiley and clingy, instead of looking like she was ready to get up and make a sandwich? Assuming royalty did such things.

"Do you know how to make a sandwich?"

"Uh, sure."

"Just checking."

He put out his right hand and rested it on her bare thigh. It *had* been an energetic twenty-five minutes. They'd wrestled all over the room, finally ending up in the middle of her king-size bed, kissing and licking and sucking and groaning. He'd held off as long as he could, which was a fucking miracle given how she'd used that soft skin and those big eyes to great effect, given how she'd stroked and teased and sighed against him.

And now they were done and . . . what? If it was any other woman, he'd get dressed and go home and promise to call her in the morning, and he always did. And they'd get together a few more times and then he'd move away, or she would, or they'd decide they weren't compatible, or they would just stop returning phone calls.

He didn't want to leave.

She yawned again. "Well, that was fun, but we both have to get up early tomorrow. Right?"

She *was* just like a guy. He didn't know whether to laugh or cry. After years of not giving a rat's ass if a girl wanted him around or not, he didn't want to leave and she couldn't wait to see him gone.

"You didn't come," he said by way of answer.

She shrugged against his shoulder. "It's all right. I had fun."

"You didn't come last time, either. I figured it was because it was so quick."

"It *was* quick," she agreed with irritating cheer.

"But now . . ."

"I don't, anymore, is all."

"Anymore?"

She sighed and crossed one knee over the other, swinging her small foot back and forth. "No, no. I had kind of a tough year last year and it's hard for me to relax . . . you know. With a gentleman."

He smiled in the dark. "Have there been that many gentlemen?"

"No you don't. I'm not touching that one with a barge pole."

"Maybe we should try again."

"It's no good, Shel. And I'm not saying this to challenge your male ego in any way. It just . . . doesn't work for me anymore."

"Not even by yourself?"

"Not even by myself."

"Since . . ." He thought about what he'd seen in the news, way back. "Since those terrorists or whatever almost killed your dad? And your brother had to take over the country? Since then?"

"I guess," she said stiffly. "I didn't mark the date on my calendar when I stopped having orgasms."

"Hmm."

"It's no big deal, Shel."

"Uh-huh."

"It really isn't."

He rubbed her thigh, thinking. "But you could come before, right?" He tried to remember how old she was. Twenty-four, twenty-five? "I mean, you weren't a virgin last year, right?"

"Right. And that's all we're saying about it."

"But—"

"Shel."

"But if you give it some thought—"

"Shel."

"I'm just saying, we could probably figure this out."

"Dr. Rivers."

"Oooh, I love it when you go all gritty and steely on me."

Thankfully, she laughed. "Shut up, you ass."

"And as a matter of fact, I do have to get up early tomorrow. Everyone has to get up early on Tuesdays. It's like a law."

"Well, then."

He sat up. "What'd you do with my pants?"

"Check over by the lamp."

"Which one? There's a hundred of them in this place." He tripped over something and stifled a curse. "And they're all off. Are you laughing? You'd better not be laughing."

"No, Dr. Rivers," she said gravely.

He finally found them and in short order had dressed, then sat on the bed to tie his shoes. "It's no trouble to stay," he said, somewhat lamely, because she obviously wanted him to leave.

"You don't have to." He could see her smiling in the gloom of the room. "I'm glad you came over."

"You'll see me again."

"Oh, that's not necessary."

He bent and kissed her. "You will, though."

He could feel her gaze on him all the way to the door.

Chapter 18

Jenny rapped on the bedroom door. Alex glanced at her watch and smiled. "Put it through," she called through the door. "And go to bed, for the love of God!"

Her bedside phone beeped. She folded the magazine in half, dropped it beside her, and picked up the phone. "I was sound asleep," she said by way of greeting.

"You lie like old people drive, m'dear."

"Hi, Dad."

"I hoped I *was* waking you up. You know what time it is there?"

"Yes, Dad."

"Well, what time is it? That wasn't rhetorical; Edmund took the clocks out of here—"

"Trying to keep you in the office during salmon season?"

"—and my damned watch stopped."

"Dad, buy a battery-operated one. Honestly. It's three-thirty."

"Damn! What's Jenny still doing up? Isn't what's-his-name, that guy we hired last year—"

"Reynolds."

"Yeah, how come he's not answering on third shift?"

"Jenny had a hot date. And, being Jenny, she can't take an evening off without punishing herself, so I guess she's pulling an all-nighter."

"Jenny had a hot *what?*"

"Dad, seriously, did you really call me in the dead of night to get all the gossip on the staff?"

"Sure. Edmund won't tell me shit."

"That's because you go around trying to fix things. I can't imagine anything worse than finding out the King of Alaska is meddling in your love life."

"Aw, shaddup. So, did I interrupt you getting ready for bed?"

"Sure," she said, humoring him.

"Liar! How can you look me in the face—so to speak—and lie like that, you little brat?"

"Well, it helps that my father is a sociopath, and my lady-in-waiting is a neurotic, tightly wound bundle of nerves with a crush—"

"Yeah? That's who she had the hot date with? The crush?"

"He's got a name, Dad," she said with exaggerated scorn, then realized that she'd forgotten it again. It wasn't an ordinary name like John. Heron? Vulture?

"Yeah, yeah. So what were you doing?"

She picked the magazine up, flipped it over, and read the cover story aloud: "Those Wacky Royals Are Just Like Us."

"We are?"

"Apparently. They got a picture of Prince Harry outside a pub—morons, like they don't know he hasn't touched a drop in two years—and there's one of David and Christina at the send-off of the Queen Mary III. God, I can't believe you talked her into that one, she's so sick of cruise ships. Oh, and here's one of Nicky on the slopes."

"Goddammit!" the king cursed. "The press was supposed to leave the kid alone on his spring break."

"It's just one candid. It's amazing—they got the names right, but not the place or the day. How do you get the place wrong when you bought the picture? I mean, you'd think the photog would say, 'FYI, I was on the Swiss Alps when I took this,' or whatever?"

"Who gives a rat shit? I'll have Edmund chew some ass."

"Come on, Dad. Besides, what was he even doing on the slopes in the first place? I thought he was in disgrace after the explosion thing."

"This happened just before. Dammit! I'll get 'em all fired, just watch."

"Dad. Relax. It's not that big a deal, why are you turning it into one? Nicky smiling, he doesn't even care. You have to admit, we don't have to put up with it nearly as much as most royals. Don't rock the boat."

"Don't *what?* Did you get mixed up and forget who you were talking to?"

"Calm down, Dad."

"A deal's a deal. They said they'd leave him alone for spring break, and I'd give 'em you for this aquarium thing. Punks!"

"Oh, very nice," she said dryly, but without heat, as that was how it worked. For all his protests, at fourteen Nicky was still a child, and the family tried to limit his dealings with the national and international press.

For her part, Alex didn't much care. They were as much a part of her life as her blue eyes and carefully chosen wardrobe. It's how things were.

"So you're lying in your bed, wide awake, reading trash about yourself at three o'clock in the morning. Is that about right?"

"According to these guys, the real reason I'm here in Minot is to cover up my raging heroin drug use."

"You're a sly one, girly. I had no idea you were a junkie."

"Can't say that anymore. And actually—I haven't been

up here alone all night. I mean, I'm alone now, but earlier—
I—I met someone, too."

"You did?" She could hear her father try to keep the
shock out of his voice. "Who is it? What's he like?"

"She, actually. I've decided men have nothing to offer
me, so now I'm a lesbian. Try to work that into your State of
the Nation speech, as a personal favor to me."

"Stop messing with my head," he ordered. "You think it's
funny, the shock at my age? And tell me about this guy."

"It's the guy I already told you about—"

"The annoying one?"

"His name's Sheldon Rivers—"

"*Shel*don?"

"Shut up, he's cool. Don't pretend you didn't read all
about him in whatever dossier Edmund made for you."

"Yeah, well, skip to the highlights."

"He's the head of the aquarium out here—"

"His name's Sheldon and he's a geek."

"His name's Sheldon and he's got a pair of shoulders like
an Olympic swimmer."

"Don't tell me this," the king groaned.

"I sweat just looking at him."

"Alex, for Christ's sake."

"You know that song 'Big John'? 'He stood six-foot-six
and weighed two forty-five . . .' "

" 'Kinda broad at the shoulder and narrow at the hip,' "
her father sang, 'everybody knew you didn't give no lip to
Big John.' Honey, who do you think played that song for
you all those years?"

"Well, I'm just saying. Sheldon's a big guy."

"For a marine weenie."

"You taken a look at your son lately? Taller than you,
isn't he?"

"Never mind," the king grumped. "Let's get back to
Shelly."

"Please promise to never call him that again."

"I'm not promising shit. Besides, it's not like I'm going to meet the guy, right?"

"Right," she said firmly. No indeed. She had no intention of letting her North Dakota fling get within a hundred miles of the king.

"So you're, what? Dating him?"

"I guess."

"Yeah, but, where's it gonna go? I mean, he knows you're not going to be around much longer, right?"

"It's not like that, Dad. We're just enjoying each other's company. He makes me laugh and I—well, I have no idea what he sees in me."

"Besides an unimaginable fortune and the chance to live in a palace."

"Trust me, that's not what it is."

"Then what *is* it? On second thought," he ordered, "don't answer that."

She giggled. "Don't worry. I love you, Dad, but some things will never be told."

"Well, I guess it's okay."

"Thank you sooooo much."

"As long as you don't enjoy it too much," her father said. "And you can consider that a royal command."

Too late, she thought, and wondered if that was smugness she felt, or something else.

Chapter 19

"This is it?" Shel asked.

"Yes."

"This is our big date?"

She almost laughed. "Yes. Why? Do you want to go back?"

"No. No, but when you said it was a surprise, and we did this mysterious long drive in a fancy RV—I mean, a family of ten could live in this place—I guess—I guess I wasn't expecting—"

There was a rap on their sitting room door, and Jenny poked her head in. "Ready to go ice fishing?" she asked cheerfully, her nose adorably red from the cold.

"This isn't ice fishing," Shel decided, following the women off the vehicle. He looked around to the small team of men and women setting up drills, equipment (depth monitors and at least one fish finder), and tables of snacks. "This is a party at the Ritz."

Alex watched indulgently as one of her guards scooped ice chips out of the most recently drilled hole (there were four altogether), and another one plunked her baited line into it, then carefully propped the rod in the snow so it wouldn't fall over. Jenny handed her a steaming cup of cocoa laced with Godiva white chocolate liqueur and she sighed.

"School coming," someone announced, gaze glued to the fish finder.

"Very well," she replied. Then, to Shel, "It's not? What else would it be? How do *you* go ice fishing?"

He waved his arms around and, in his dark brown parka and matching snowpants, looked like an irked koala. "Not like this! Not with fifty people driving me and drilling my hole and giving me snacks!"

"But it's so nice this way," Alex pointed out, and took a sip. "Mmm . . . Godiva up this drink a little more, will you, Jenn? Look, if you don't like it, go back into the RV and have a nap."

"I'm not . . . never mind. Where *are* we, anyway?"

"Manitoba. It's a little too far into spring in Minot to do this safely," she said, gesturing to all the vehicles parked on the ice. She grinned at him. "Don't pretend you minded the drive."

"It's not the drive that's weirding me out. It's—"

"Your Highness, you've got a bite."

"It's that!" Shel nearly shouted, watching another staff member crouch over the hole, gently pick up the rod, set the hook, and pull a wriggling, thirteen-inch Northern Pike onto the ice. "That! That is not ice fishing! That is watching someone fish! I might as well be watching this on TV!"

"Dr. Rivers has a bite," someone else announced.

"The hell I do! And I'm not landing it, either!"

"That's all right," Jenny said cheerfully, trying to hand him a cup of coffee. "We'll take care of it."

"Another pike," one of the guides said, pulling the addled fish onto the ice. "A little too small; we'll unhook this feller and put him back. And the princess has another bite."

"We're in the school," the gal with her face in the monitor announced, unnecessarily.

"Nice fish," Reynolds, the guard, told him.

"It's not my fish! And it was just a baby."

"You'll get another one," Alex said, comforting him.

"No I won't! Aren't you listening?"

"It's hard to listen when you do all that shouting. I thought you'd like this. I thought this would be right up your alley," she complained. "God knows standing around freezing my ass off isn't my idea of a fun afternoon."

"How can being waited on hand and toe not be your idea of a fun afternoon? You're not even cold!"

"Dr. Rivers has another bite."

"No! I! Don't!" They were all staring at him as he shrieked. Fearing he might pop an aneurysm, he stomped up the steps into the waiting RV.

"**W**ell!" Alex said brightly, shrugging out of her outer winter clothes and dismissing Jenny with a wave of her hand. "That was quite a show you put on this afternoon."

"Look, we just have different ideas about ice fishing, that's all. I was . . . surprised. Uh, pleasantly surprised."

"Mmm-hmm. I suppose your idea of fun is to crouch, shivering, over a hole it took you an hour to dig with substandard equipment, and no snacks, and no shelter if the wind picks up, and nothing to tell you if the fish are anywhere around."

"I can't help it," he bragged, "if I fish like a man."

She laughed at him and rubbed her eyes at the same time. "Well, I'm glad to be back at the hotel at least. God, I miss my bed."

"Are you all right?"

"Why, do I look like hell?"

"You look a little . . ." Sheldon was studying her with a gaze as alarming as it was penetrating. "Hollow-eyed."

"I was up all night talking to my dad. And then, of course, there was the fun-filled afternoon with Dr. Grumpy."

"Oh yeah? He calls you?"

"When I'm on the road. He's kind of a mother hen."

"The King of Alaska? I've seen pictures. The phrase 'mother hen' doesn't exactly leap to my mind. I mean, he's got fists the size of coconuts! That's just a scary, scary thought."

"Well, you know. He worries. It's been just him since my mother died, and I was just a kid when that happened, so . . ." She trailed off. Where was she going with that? It was hard to keep hold of a thought. She estimated she had slept ten hours in the last one hundred and twenty. It was easier to sleep when she knew Dara was safe, from—from— Her tired mind groped, lost it, tried again, gave up. "So it's just us. I mean, us and my brothers and my sister. He bugs them, too."

"Uh-huh. I have this keen idea."

"Keen?" She smiled a little. "Jeepers, Dr. Rivers, I can't wait to hear all about your nifty plan."

"You're so grouchy when you're tired. And my keen plan is this: let's bag dinner and take a nap instead."

"That's all right," she said, walking over to the mirror on the wall. "I got my fifteen minutes this afternoon. Good God, I look embalmed."

He laughed, came up behind her, and put his hands on her shoulders. She leaned back, enjoying the feel of him, the smell. "Princess, on your worst day you look like a movie star on her best."

"Dark circles and all."

"They're sexy."

"So's foot fungus."

"Uh, no."

"You know what I like about you?" she asked his reflection in the mirror.

"My wit, my sparkling personality? My gigantic cock?"

"None of those."

"Well, shit."

"I like that you're not trying to impress me all the time. I mean, look what you're wearing. Dockers, and no socks! Most people in a private meeting with royalty would put on socks, at least."

"They're all in the wash, along with most of my underpants. Come on." He took her by the hand and pulled her into the bedroom.

"Well, finally. I didn't think we were ever going to get down to it."

"For an untouchable royal princess, you've got a shocking one-track mind. Lie down."

"Sit," she said, lying down. "Stay. Roll over."

"Look, I will, too, okay?"

"Roll over?"

He ignored the obvious crack. "We'll just have a nap."

"And then all my problems will be solved! Thank goodness for your little plan. Shel, I've tried this. It doesn't work. I can't nap."

"Yes you can. Just close your eyes and go to sleep."

"No, I mean it. Even when I didn't have insomnia. I can't sleep during the day."

"Yes you can."

"Shel! Jesus, did you really think I wouldn't have thought of this if the great Dr. Rivers hadn't come along?"

"Can I get that on a T-shirt? 'The Great Dr. Rivers'?"

"I've tried this stuff, okay? It doesn't work. I can't nap."

"Look, I'm not asking you to cure bone cancer, for crying out loud, just take a nap at five o'clock." He propped himself up on his side and rubbed her arm, then began to sing in a cracking baritone, "Go to sleeeeeeep . . . goooooo to sleeeeeeep . . ."

"How in the hell am I supposed to sleep with that racket?" she bitched. "Yet another flaw: you sing like old people drive. I'm keeping a list, you know."

". . . I'm ignoring you . . . gooooo to sleep . . ."

"Stop singing," she said, "and I'll close my eyes."

"Done and done."

Forty minutes later . . .

"Can I get up now?"

"How could you not sleep?" he demanded, looming over her. "You did that on purpose!"

"Yes, I really get off on irritability, memory loss, loss of appetite, and all the other fun effects of long-term insomnia. Also, I'm conducting a survey, and it doesn't matter how many channels you have, there is nothing on at four in the morning."

"Well, that would not fucking surprise me!" he shouted, sitting up. "Who lies in a sumptuous royal suite, getting sung to sleep on a feather bed with expensive pillows and all that fancy shit, and doesn't sleep?"

"It's all part of my sinister plan."

He stomped around the bedroom for a minute, and she got up to brush her hair, amused. He really seemed genuinely annoyed that his plan hadn't worked. Men! She admired their confidence: *I can fix it, just give me a minute.*

"Well, hell," he said after muttering and grumbling. "I guess we'd better have dinner, then."

"Those were our only choices?" she teased. "Nap or eat?"

"Well . . ." He crossed the room and went to his navy-blue backpack. Which was odd, as she'd never seen him with one before. And it was strangely deflated, as if there weren't very many things inside. "I did have one idea . . ."

"Did you bring some Ritz? Because I *am* a little hungry . . . one nice thing about being on the road is I don't have to wait until eight o'clock to eat supper." She blinked. "What the hell?"

He held up something shiny, something the light bounced off of. Handcuffs.

Chapter 20

"**W**hy, Dr. Rivers," she said, staring.

"Now, it's not what you think," he began.

"Really? It's not? Because I'm thinking you're a man just full of surprises."

"Okay, thanks." He was still holding the cuffs up, watching them spin lazily. "What I was afraid you were thinking was that I was some big old perv."

She laughed nervously. "No, I wasn't thinking that."

"Okay, and I know it's a big step for us, and you more than most people have to worry about, you know, the Paris Hilton effect and all that—"

"You've got a video camera in there?" She tried to figure out if she was horrified, or interested. "I'm dying to see what else you carry around with you."

"No! No no no. I'd never ask you to do that. Do it on camera, I mean. Like I said, you more than most people would have to worry about it getting out. Although these things don't just 'get out'," he added in a mutter. "The asshole ex-boyfriend sells her out, is what—okay, we're getting off the subject."

"And the subject was bondage?" She sat on the edge of the bed and looked up at him like an attentive pupil.

"Uh, yeah. And a change of clothes."

"What? Sorry, I'm having a little trouble following you."

"In my pack." He held the bag open and showed her; she could see a glimpse of white cotton, denim, and buttercup yellow. "I got you some souvenir T-shirts."

She laughed. "Thank you."

"Welcome. I also brought a change of clothes. In case you, uh, we decided to spend the night. That I could spend the night."

"One thing at a time, doctor. I'm pretty sure," she mused, "that I don't know you well enough to let you cuff me to the headboard."

"That reminds me." He dug through the pack and she heard the clink as he held up the second pair. "Okay, don't freak out, but because it's a headboard, we need two pairs. Otherwise you're lying on your hands and I don't think that'd be very comfortable."

"You seem to know a lot about it," she observed.

He blushed. Blushed like a kid! His cheeks went red and his eyes seemed to get darker. "I've never done this before. It just seemed logical, the hand thing. You're the only girl I ever wanted to tie up."

"Oh, Dr. Rivers!" To cover her extreme nervousness, she folded her hands over her breasts and looked up at him adoringly, batting her eyelashes. "That's so sweet."

To her relief, he laughed, and some of the high color left his cheeks. "Yeah, yeah, very funny. But I really haven't."

"In that case, I'm dying to know . . . where did you get two pairs of stainless steel handcuffs in Minot? You didn't—" She nearly vomited as the thought struck her. "You didn't ask my security team for them, d—"

"No. God, no, I'd never do that. Didn't I just get done telling you I was sensitive to your needs, as a celebrity, not to be sexually embarrassed on the World Wide Web? Or anywhere?"

"So where did you get them?" she asked, calming down.

He grinned at her. "Some things," he vowed, "will never be told. Suffice it to say, there are some interesting people frequenting the sex shop in this town."

"And I bet they all have doctorates."

"I'm assuming, from all the joking, that you haven't done this with anyone either?"

"Not hardly," she said, watching him spin the cuffs on the end of his right index finger. "I was nervous enough about losing my virginity, and I was nineteen when I got around to *that*."

"Well, here's what I'm thinking. Think fast." He tossed her a pair and she caught them by reflex. Out of pure curiosity she studied them. Yes indeed, stainless steel and very sturdy. "I think it's a control issue. With you. And not coming."

"Oh boy," she said, flopping back down on the bed.

"Hear me out! I think if you gave up a little bit of control, you might have a better time. That's all. It's an experiment. If it works, great. And if it doesn't—"

"You got a money-back guarantee?"

He laughed. "No. I guess I'll throw them away if it doesn't work."

"Shel." She sighed. "I told you it wasn't a problem for you to fix."

"Well, I'm a fixer," he said cheerfully. "I figured, we start out slow, and if you don't like it, we're done."

She studied the cuffs again. "I can't believe I'm even thinking about this."

"Well, you're right in that we haven't known each other very long, but how many girls have a team of highly-trained bodyguards in the next suite, ready to kick the living shit out of me if I forget the safety word?"

She burst out laughing. "I hadn't thought about it like that."

"Which is *Dendrochirus zebra*, by the way."

"What?"

"The safety word." At her confused (possibly aghast) expression, he hurried to explain. "You know, in case one of us takes it too far by accident. It's got to be a word you wouldn't use in everyday conversation."

"Everyday conversation! What the hell does it even mean?"

"It's the Latin name for zebra lionfish," he explained, in an "everybody knows that" tone.

"How about just zebra? I don't use that too much in everyday conversation."

"Well, okay, I guess, if you think—" He did a comical double-take, just like in an old comedy. "You want to? You'll give it a try?"

"Yeah, why not? Being cuffed isn't as scary as trying to remember *Dendrochirus zebra*." *Or watching your father get shot*, a tiny voice in her mind spoke up, and she stomped on it like a bug, made it gone. "You had a point about my guards, anyway. Try anything fishy, and you're shot, clubbed, or stabbed. Possibly all three."

"That's so romantic. And it's *DEN-drochirus*," he whispered, taking her in his arms.

Chapter 21

By the time they had stripped and he had carefully cuffed each of her wrists to a section of the barred headboard, she was shocked to realize how excited she was. And when he slipped a hand between her thighs, he was shocked too, she saw at once, and the blood rushed to his face again—but not out of embarrassment. No indeed.

Then she couldn't see his face any longer as it disappeared between her legs, as he licked and kissed away the wetness she had made, they had made. His tongue was stabbing into her; it was like a knife that didn't hurt, one made of sweet darkness, one she felt all over.

She could feel his bristly cheeks—he hadn't shaved that day—rubbing against her inner thighs, felt his hands stroking her outer thighs, rubbing them restlessly, ceaselessly.

So much for starting out slow, she thought, and that made it more exciting, which she hadn't thought possible. That he couldn't. That they couldn't. That he'd dived between her legs and she didn't mind, that he hadn't gone near her breasts or her mouth and she didn't mind, that she was about to . . . to . . .

No, she didn't do that anymore, it was further off, it was

a trick, just her body tricking her again, making her think she would sleep, making her think she wouldn't dream, making her think she could come with just a minute of tongue and stainless steel, no, she wouldn't, she . . . was . . . coming.

She screamed and groaned at the same time, shoving herself closer to his mouth, his dark sweet mouth, and he stabbed her, he stabbed her, he was . . . coming up between her legs, his broad chest settling against hers, his hands on her thighs, spreading them apart, and he slipped into her like she was made of oil and she screamed again, into his mouth, screamed and thought *oh I am dying.*

He shuddered against her and she wrapped her legs around him and held on, and felt her long-gone friend, that black flower, blossom inside her once more.

"Oh, Christ!" he cried, and she knew his friend had come for him, too.

Chapter 22

"Christ," he said again.

"Sing it."

"That was—"

"Testify."

"I can't believe—"

"*You* can't believe?"

"I mean, you were *so* wet. And I was totally ready. I was going to blow up all over you if you weren't ready, I swear to God."

"What a charming thought." She laughed. Then she shocked herself (and him) by bursting into tears.

"Oh, Alex—"

"Unhook me," she sobbed.

"Sure, sweetie, right now." He had the keys in his hand in half an instant, and in two clicks she was free and he was holding her. "Did you, uh, forget—"

"No, I didn't forget the stupid fucking safety word, *Dendrochirus zebra*, there, are you fucking happy?"

"Sure, honey. It's all right."

"I don't even know why I'm crying!"

"Okay."

"Because I just had a great time, everything's great! And I'm not upset about *anything*."

"Okay, hon. Okay."

"It's just that I'm tired," she wept.

"Of course you are. And hungry. We skipped supper and I didn't bring any Ritz, remember?"

"Some kind of lousy date you are," she said, snuggling into him as he kissed her tears away.

Much later, after she'd gotten hold of herself, she said, "Now, don't be smug."

"Never."

"I mean it! You're radiating 'I cured her I'm so smart' vibes and it's going to really tick me off."

"That was a great time," he sighed, staring at the ceiling. He had laced his hands together behind his head, and she was resting the heel of one of her feet on his left knee. "Really, really great."

"Really, really?" she teased. "That's some vocabulary you've got, Dr. Rivers."

"And I'm spending the night, so just freak out about it now and get it over with."

"Uh . . ."

"Alex."

"It's just . . . if someone gets a picture of you on the way out tomorrow . . ."

"So?"

"Well, they'll print stories about you. And chances are, none of them will be true."

"So?"

So indeed. Did she care? The press would jump to inane, incorrect assumptions, but that was their job, and she didn't mind, did she?

No, it was the spending the night thing. *That* she minded.

"Look, Alex, I don't give a crap if the *Minot Daily News* puts my picture on the front page, or even the back page. Or if they sell the pic to *People* or whoever. I really don't care. I just want to be with you, okay? I don't want to fuck and run."

"Well," she lied, "I don't want you to."

"Oh." He'd clearly been expecting more resistance, but she couldn't think of a way to make him leave without hurting his feelings. And after the gift he'd just given her, it would seem . . . churlish. To send him away. To sleep alone. Not that she would sleep, of course. At least, not for long.

"I'm just saying," he said, picking up one of her hands and kissing the palm, "I'm looking for more than a good time with you, that's all."

He was heartless, the way he terrified her! What a cool bastard. Unless he wasn't trying to scare her. Which was even more terrifying. "Well, thanks," she said, aware of how lame it sounded, but completely unable to think of a more appropriate response.

Chapter 23

"**N**icky! *Nicky, get down!*"

Hands on her, shaking her. Not hurting her. Where was the gun?

My father is the true king.

You've fucked up, it's done.

You shot my daddy.

Don't worry, Nicky.

"Nicky!"

I'm going to fix him. I'm going to fix everything.

"Alex, will you wake. The fuck. Up."

She opened her eyes and said to the dark, "He's not dead. Not really."

"He sure is, sweetie. The way I heard the story, you bashed his brains in."

It was Sheldon. In the dark. With her. Had she—

"Oh, God," she groaned. She tried to cover her face, but he gripped her wrists and held them, gently but firmly. "I'm so embarrassed! Did I wake you? Was I *screaming?*" She could not have been more humiliated if he'd hit her. "I never do that, never! I—"

"Hey, it's all right." Lie. She could see, now that her eyes had adjusted to the dark, the beads of sweat on his forehead. She'd scared him, and badly. "I'm just glad you're awake. Which is an awful thing to say to an insomniac, I know."

"I can't believe I—let go." He did, and she sat up and observed her hands were shaking. "I can't—believe I did that. I'm so sorry. I didn't—"

"Alex, it's no big! Will you just relax? I've seen the look on your face when you come, tied you up, had my tongue in your mouth and everywhere else, *and* used your toothbrush, but you're embarrassed about this?"

"Extremely," she said hollowly.

"God, what a moment!" He scrubbed his face with his hands. "Look, it's no big deal, it was just sort of terrifying to be sound asleep and then hear you practically screaming. I mean, I was looking for a bunch of Marines or zombies or something."

"Don't remind me."

"That's why you can't sleep? You keep having the same dream over and—"

"I don't want to talk about it."

"Well, too bad." He said it reasonably enough, and she glared at him. "Look, it's not like we can roll over and go back to sleep, right? I mean, you're probably done for the night . . ." He squinted at his watch. "You got all of an hour and a half. And frankly, my pulse is about one-eighty right now from the adrenaline rush. So let's talk about this."

"I have a shrink, Shel. Your duties are entirely different."

His brow wrinkled. "Duties?"

Yes! Offend him and he'll leave! "You heard me."

"Okay, whatever. Listen, getting back to this recurring nightmare—"

Dammit! "Sheldon, aren't you insulted? I just implied you're about as important to me as my father's footmen."

"You can't pick a fight and get rid of me that easily," he said with irritating smugness.

"Well, we're not talking about me unless you tell me deep dark secrets about you." He was, in his own way, as closed off as she was, and surely this would—

"Done. I hate royalty, inherited wealth, brunettes, and cheese."

She was utterly distracted. "What? You *hate* them? Brunettes and cheese? Why?"

"Your turn. Why do you think you keep having that dream?"

She paused a moment, but a deal was a deal. And she just had to hear about the cheese. "Well, according to my shrink, it was the first time in my life, my very scheduled and controlled life, that something happened that was completely beyond my control. I fixed it, but it might not have worked. It might have ended even worse than it did. That's what haunts me. Not what I did. What could have happened. My little brother—my king! And Chris and—and—she might have been pregnant at the time, so Dara would have—it could have been so much worse. And might be. Someday. Because maybe next time I can't fix it. You know?"

"What about—I don't mean this in a mean way, but what about when your mom died? Car accident, right? You couldn't control that, either."

"Yes, but it didn't happen right in front of my face. I wasn't even there. And everything that happened after—the mass, the funeral, the burial, the visitations—was scheduled. Controlled. And I—I didn't see much of her. When she was alive, I didn't . . ." She paused. "Now, about cheese."

"Have you ever seen a slice of artisanal cheese under a microscope?" He shuddered. Actually shivered like a kid hiding from a storm. "It's alive! That's why you're not supposed to wrap the good stuff in plastic wrap. It suffocates. It's alive!"

"Okay, okay," she soothed, because he looked ready to leap off the bed and out the window. A bad choice from six stories up. "Well, we won't serve any of it. Not even the cheap stuff."

"It moves," he said darkly. "It *wiggles*."

"That's terrible," she said, totally straight-faced. Her years of poker playing were serving her well. Cheese! Ha! "And what have you got against brunettes?"

"Oh, the gal who turned me down for prom had brown hair, and I had a huge crush on her, and I'd been screwing up my courage for, like, two years, waiting to be old enough, and she turned me down flat. So ever since then I've tried to stick to blondes and redheads. But in your case, I made an exception."

"Thank you so much. And what about—"

"My turn, thanks. Did you, uh, have to go to jail or even get arrested or . . ." The amused look on her face was answer enough. "Okay, dumb question. I guess when you kill a guy defending your country and the monarch, they overlook manslaughter."

"They do," she said soberly. "If I hadn't killed him, he would have been beheaded. That's still the law on the books in my country."

"Civilized."

"More so than the electric chair," she snapped. "You Americans! 'Our way is the best way and if you don't like it, move over.' Very nice!"

"Okay, okay, let's not get into that . . . I mean, we can't help being the greatest country in the world, but that's not—"

"I bet I know why you don't like inherited wealth."

"Go ahead, Dr. Freud."

"You said you were an Army brat, right? So virtually everything your family made in terms of money was paid by taxes, right?"

"Well, not exactly—"

"So here's your family, defending your country and getting paid next to nothing to do the job, while the rich ass-holes who are supposed to pay their fair share of taxes get a million shelters and only pay a fraction of what they owe. Right? That's how it is in this country, isn't it?"

"More or less," he said grudgingly. "It's a little more complicated than that."

"We have a flat tax in Alaska," she explained, trying not to sound smug.

"Well, bully for Alaska."

"Everybody pays exactly the same percentage. It works out really well. If you came to visit—if you ever wanted to come—you'd see the roads and bridges and hospitals are all in good shape. We've got plenty of money for infrastructure."

"Well. I'm pretty busy here. I—I'd like to visit but I'm not sure when I could—"

"Forget it." She paused. "Wow."

"What?"

"I'm impressed, is all. I mean, you weren't kidding around when we first met. You *really* didn't like me. I might as well have been wearing a cheese bikini."

"It sort of took me by surprise," he admitted. "You being so pretty and funny and fearless. I was expecting a snob who wouldn't talk to anyone."

"It's irresistible," she said, pouncing on him, "that you didn't like me."

"I think," he said as she leaned down to nibble on his mouth, "you should up your visits to the shrink."

"Oh, shut up," she mumbled.

Chapter 24

Two days later, Jenny brought in the paper along with the usual morning correspondence. Alex was not surprised to see Dr. Sheldon Rivers glaring up at her from page one.

"Here we go," she muttered.

"He looks like Sean Penn from the old days," Jenny said admiringly, peeking over her shoulder. "Like he's about to belt one of the photogs."

It's his anti-cheese glare, she thought with a silent snicker. Aloud, she added, "It had been a long night." And an even longer day. And night. Sheldon had some stupid out-of-town conference for geeks he couldn't get out of. So she hadn't seen him, in fact, since the night of the nightmare. Well, the nightmare he interrupted. It was awful, how much she missed him.

Awful. In about five different ways.

"And Princess Christina called again."

Alex shook her head. "I'm in no mood for one of her lectures, Jenny. Keep telling her I'm out."

"Yes, Princess." This in a voice of doom.

"Jenny, I'm sorry."

"Nothing to be sorry for, Your Highness."

"I know she squawks and yells and knows you're lying and screams and gives you a headache."

"It's part of my job, Highness," Jenny said bravely, unconsciously massaging her temples.

"Well, I really appreciate it. If it makes you feel better, I feel loads of guilt every time I dodge a call and make you take the fall for it."

Jenny perked up. "Thank you, Highness."

"You're taking the evening off, right? Giving someone else phone duty? Relieving my constant, nagging guilt?"

"Yes, Mr. Grange is taking me bowling."

Alex felt her mouth pop open. "He is?"

"I want to go," she said defensively.

"Jenny."

"Well, *he* wanted to go. And I don't mind. I've never ever been. Imagine! Rented shoes and—and—beer in—in—disposable cups."

Alex almost smiled at the revolted look on the other woman's face. "I'm sure it will be swell. Jenny, did you bring jeans? Or at least slacks?"

"I have a skirt that's an inch above my knee," she said slowly.

"Whoa, slut on the loose! Look, go through my closet and grab a pair of jeans, willya?"

"Thank you, but I'll have enough trouble learning the game without tripping over five inch cuffs."

"Then I strongly advise you to take some time this afternoon and go shopping. You don't want to learn how to bowl in a skirt."

"Thank you, Highness, I will take that advice. Now, back to business. According to this," she said, tapping the newspaper, "you and Dr. Rivers have been working on the plans for the new wing in your private chambers. Implying, of course, that you're really just having sex."

"Which, of course, we are."

"Yes. But they're very careful. They're letting the readers jump to conclusions, instead of leading them by the nose."

"The conservative Midwest?" Alex suggested.

"Or they've been sued so now they're careful. Either way, Dr. Rivers won't be pleased, though there isn't anything too damaging here. Unless you realize the picture was taken at four A.M. outside your hotel."

"I warned him. He said he didn't care."

"Very good, Princess. I take it there will be no official response to this?"

"If we got caught with his hand up my skirt, that's my fault, and I'm sure not going imply the newspaper lied."

"As long as Dr. Rivers understands . . ." She paused delicately.

"Well, like I said. I did tell him."

"Very good."

"I guess we'll find out if he meant it."

"Yes. I imagine we will."

"He should get some warning, though, don't you think? I mean, he's not used to this kind of thing at all. Maybe I'll bring it over to his office this afternoon," Alex suggested. "Sort of muffle the shock. He never reads the paper, anyway. I could probably get it to him first. Warn him, you know?"

"I think that's an excellent idea, Princess," Jenny said gravely. "You've got some room in your schedule today. Perhaps you should meet him at the airport and ensure no one else shows him the paper first."

"I could, but . . . I don't have his flight information. And he's the only guy on the planet who refuses to turn on his cell phone."

Jenny smiled. "With all due respect, Your Highness, you don't think much of your staff, do you?"

Chapter 25

Pick 'n' Pin
Five hours later

"**D**amn that ball anyway!"

"Easy, cutie," Teal said. He was still holding the paper and grinning admiringly at the scowling photo of his best friend. "Everybody has a hard time at first. Shit, that's how I found out I needed glasses. I kept throwing my ball down the wrong damn lane."

"You're lying," she said, puffing a strand of hair out of her face and stomping back to the small cubby where they were keeping score, "to comfort me. Thank you."

"Hey, you're doing great for your first time! And I gotta say," he added with a friendly leer, "I love you in blue jeans."

"They're new," she said, pleased. "I went to Target. Her Highness insisted."

"Her Highness knows her shit. You look great."

"I dread your reunion with Dr. Rivers," she teased. "Since you appear to be carrying that newspaper wherever you go today."

"I can't help it. I never knew anybody important enough to be on the front page before. In a good way, I mean. But that's a whole other story. Man!" He smoothed the paper and added admiringly, "I cannot believe Shel's in the paper. Because he's knocking boots with the friggin' Princess of Alaska!"

"Umm," Jenny said noncommittally.

"I can't even believe they're dating," he continued, getting up and plucking a new ball from the steadily growing pile. "Shel hates rich people. I mean, *hates* 'em."

"How can he hate a class of people most of whom he's never likely to meet?"

"Because he's a weirdo."

"He seemed . . . prickly . . . when we first met at the Aquarium," she said carefully.

"Yeah, your tact's in overdrive today, honey. He was *so* pissed when he heard you were coming and that his boss wanted him to play tour guide. I can't even believe he did it."

"He got a good look at her," Jenny guessed. "It happens to a lot of men."

"Y'know, he didn't have much money as a kid and rich people really torqued him off. Said his dad busted his ass for practically minimum wage, and as thanks they kept sending him overseas when he was practically an old man."

"His father didn't like that?"

"His father *loved* it. That's the whole problem. His old man was an adrenalin junkie, and traveled all over the world setting up triage centers—he was Dr. Rivers, too, only an M.D. Never around, I mean *never*."

"Really?"

Teal seemed to realize what he was doing, because he rolled a strike, then turned and shrugged. "Sorry. Here I'm spending our whole date gossiping about my friend."

"It's interesting."

"Yeah, and it's all going into a memo to your boss, I bet."

"It certainly will not!"

"Oh. Sorry."

"I mean," she added, "I might mention it in passing, over a cup of coffee, but not if you asked me to keep a confidence."

"Oh." He considered that for a long moment, taking off his glasses and polishing them on his cherry red flannel shirt. "Well, I guess I'll leave it up to you to decide what to pass on and what not to."

"Thank you." Then, because she couldn't help herself: "You know, that's terrible for the lenses."

"Never mind. Anyway—here's your ball. His dad was never around for Christmas, birthdays, Thanksgiving . . . I mean never. And Shel hated it. And his mom hated it. And all his sibs hated it. Everybody but Dr. Rivers, I guess."

"So instead of blaming his father for an overly developed work-ethic—"

"Ha! You'd know about that, huh, Jenn?"

"—he chose instead to blame the wealthy?"

"Something like that. You know, something that makes him sound like less of a dick. That's why I was so surprised when they seemed to, you know, hit it off. It'd be your classic poor-boy-falls-for-rich-girl story, except for how he hates rich people. And royalty. And brunettes. You know, because of the prom. But that's a whole other thing."

"Indeed." She rolled her ball with a grunt, and watched, surprised, as three pins were knocked over.

"There ya go!"

"At this rate, I can roll three hundred in . . . oh, dear, I just gave myself a headache."

"Don't be so hard on yourself. It's a date, hon, the word is fun."

"Is that the word?"

"Yeah, and we're not going to spend all night talking about your boss and my best friend, are we?"

"I had planned on it," she admitted, making sure her brown turtleneck was tucked in all the way around. Some of her bowls took a bit out of her.

"Hon, you've gotta take a vacation."

"Hon, that's what everyone keeps telling me."

Chapter 26

The cuffs were rattling in her ears as she clung to the wooden bars of the headboard, facedown on the mattress. Shel pushed into her from behind with a sound that was halfway between a grunt and a moan. She tried to get up on her knees a bit to meet his thrusts, but with a hand in the middle of her back he pushed her back down and thrust deeply, sweetly.

She felt him filling her up, felt his hot breath on the back of her neck, heard his groans. He shifted, and then one hand was in her hair and the other was clenched in a fist on the pillow beside her as he worked her from behind, treated himself at the same time, rubbed, touched, fucked. And oh, Christ, she loved it, it was *ridiculous* how much she loved it, how good it felt, his hands, his dick, his lips pressed tightly against her left shoulder.

She could feel her orgasm approach like a roaring freight train, and gripped the bars so hard her knuckles whitened. Then she was coming, coming so hard she could actually feel her uterus contracting, and he was gasping and shifting behind her, pushing, stroking, and just when the train slowed down it sped up again, taking her with it, and she let go of the bars as he stiffened behind her and groaned her name into her hair.

"Ah, God," she gasped after a long moment.

"Killing me," he mumbled. "You're killing me. Don't think I don't know. It's a plot. You're trying to take over my country—"

"One marine biologist at a time. Now that you've figured it out, I'll *have* to kill you."

"You are," he said, smiling, as he got up and unlocked her.

One thing they had agreed on: the cuffs were for sex. Nothing else. No pre-copulation taunting, no post-coital chatting with her arms over her head. The keys were kept right beside them and, for safety's sake, he had a spare set in the pocket of his backpack. No wacky "jeepers, I can't find the key I guess we'd better call a locksmith" hijinks for her, thank you very much.

It was funny . . . she loved being restricted while they were fucking, and absolutely could not tolerate it when they weren't.

She must have spoken aloud, because she heard him say, "Fucking? Oh, that's a nice word. Is that what we're doing?"

"Forget it," she told him, rubbing her wrists. They weren't sore, but it was good to have freedom of movement again. "I hate the word 'lovemaking.' I always picture some-one knitting."

"Knitting love?"

"Seriously, Shel. I hate that word."

"Mmm." He grabbed her wrist and examined it, then grabbed the other one, satisfied himself there were no marks, and let go. "Sex, then? Because I'm not too fond of 'fucking' unless somebody's swearing."

"Why?"

"It sounds cold," he said shortly. "Like what we're doing

in here doesn't mean anything. Like it could be anybody in here."

"Sex it is," she agreed, ignoring the stab of anxiety his words brought. "You know, Dr. Rivers, when we met, I never dreamed you were the type to get so easily attached."

She had tried to make a joke out of it, but he didn't crack a smile. "I'm not," he said shortly. "But—"

Then, thank God, the phone rang. Alex reached for it. Lunged for it, truth be told.

"Come on," he protested. "You're on your own time. It's almost midnight, for crying out loud."

"I know. But Terry wouldn't bug me this late unless it was important." *And frankly, I've had about as much of this awkward conversation as I'm going to take.* "Hello?"

"Your Highness, this is Reynolds."

"Yes, Terry, what can I do for you?"

"I'm really sorry to bother you so late, but I've got Princess Christina on the other line. She says Princess Dara is sick."

Oh Jesus. "Put her through. And then call my pilot and tell him to be ready to go back home."

"At once, Your Highness." There was the temporary black hole of being on hold and she saw Shel pull his shirt on out of the corner of her eye.

"What's wrong?" he whispered, stepping into his boxers.

"My niece is sick. Hello?"

"Alex?"

"Chris, what—"

"Listen. It was a shitty thing to do and I apologize, and it's important that you get this: Dara's fine. Okay? She's totally fine. Pooped twice today, in fact. We're still reeling from it."

"Wh—why—"

"Look, I'm really sorry, I just didn't see any way around it. You've been dodging my calls—"

"Christina."

"And don't get all snotty and royal on me, either! Believe me, you'll thank me for this. He's on his way."

"What?" She was so relieved the baby was safe, she was having trouble following. "Who? What?"

"Aren't you supposed to be the smart one? Your dad! King Al! He saw the paper—you can kick Edmund's ass for that one, by the way—and totally flipped out. Signed a bunch of crap and came out on his plane as soon as he could. I didn't even know he'd left until I practically beat it out of Edmund, that rat fink."

"He's on his way here?"

"No, I'm mean he's there right *now*."

!!!

"Alex? Hello?"

"Oh, God."

"Exactly. So, honey, if you've, you know, got a friend up there, now would be a real good time to give him the boot, get me?"

Alex swayed as the full, awful dreadfulness of the moment swept over her. She was frozen in place like any heroine in a bad horror movie. Her mind shouted a hundred directions, but she just stood there, dimly hearing Christina squawk through the receiver.

"What's wrong?" Sheldon asked again, just as the door shook. As if someone with coconut-size hands was knocking on it, and in a hurry.

Chapter 27

"Hi, Dad!" she said, giving the king her brightest smile as she swung the door open. She tightened the belt on her robe, then nearly went sprawling as her father marched past her.

"Got some good staff downstairs," he commented. "You wouldn't believe the shit they were shoveling in order to stop me from coming up."

"What shit?" she asked innocently, raking a hand through her hair.

"Apparently, you're drunk, with a migraine, and going into withdrawal from the heroin treatment, and can't have visitors. To my own face they're telling me this! I could have them imprisoned for fifty years!"

"I am getting a bit of a headache," she admitted.

"My ass you are." He was looking around the suite, then spotted Shel. His blue eyes went narrow and squinty and he lunged forward.

So did Alex, wrapping her arms around his (slightly thickened) middle. The tops of her feet dragged across the lush carpet as he dragged her a meter and a half, then gave up.

"For Christ's sake, Alex. Leggo."

She did, thudding to the carpet, then leaping to her feet before her father or Shel could help her up. "Dad, I'm warning you."

His eyes went wide, and the corner of his mouth turned up in an expression she knew well: He was pissed, but trying not to laugh. "You're warning me? Sweetheart, you might want to check the history books. I've got rank."

"Dad, I'm serious. Don't you touch him. Not one finger, not one knuckle. I'm twenty-five years old, for God's sake!"

"Yeah, and I've been telling you for about that long to watch out for fortune hunters," he snapped back. "This kid doesn't have a penny to his—"

"Fortune hunters?" Shel repeated, sounding like he'd found a snake in the toilet. Alex groaned and made frantic throat-slashing motions, to no avail. "Not fucking likely! What, you think that's the only reason someone would be interested in your daughter?"

"Who's talking to you, boy?"

"Because it's not, mister! King! Whatever! She's smart and sexy and funny and chilly and tough and—"

"Quiet, you. Alex, what the hell? I gotta read this in the papers?"

"It's not like that, Dad."

"What's it like, then?"

"Private. That's what it's like."

"You didn't tell him *anything* about us?" Now Sheldon sounded as if the snake in the toilet had hatched babies in his shoes.

"I did! Remember, Dad, on the phone the other—"

"Yeah, yeah. Get some pants on, boy," the king ordered. "Then join me outside."

" 'Join me' better not be a euphemism for 'let me beat you until you need a cast,' " Alex warned.

"You could stand to put some pants on, too," the king said, mildly enough, and then stepped out of the room.

Chapter 28

"Sir," Jenny said nervously, "you have to admit, she's sleeping better."

"Yeah, real novel way to fight insomnia," the king snapped.

Alex laughed and, when the king scowled more, laughed harder. Shel, who had been trying to remember if it was against the law to have sex with a member of the Alaskan family out of wedlock, did a double take. He had so rarely heard her laugh like that . . . uncomplicated and joyous.

"You hypocrite," she said, ignoring Jenny's blanch. "You're not going to pretend you went to your wedding bed a virgin. Did you even make it into your late teens? How many royal bastards are running around?"

"You hypocrite, *Your Majesty*. I also answer to 'my king'. And we're not talking about me, we're talking about you. I'm in my—well, I'm not a kid anymore, but you are."

"I'm a quarter of a century old, Dad. When you were my age, you were married and had kids."

The king ignored her impeccable logic, turning again to the cringing brunette who looked as if she wished to be anywhere, anywhere but in that room. "Jenny, you're killin' me. You're supposed to keep an eye on her! Are those blue jeans?"

Jenny blushed so hard, Shel thought she was going to have an aneurysm on the spot. "My king, they are. I was enjoying a private engagement earlier when I was made aware of—of your joyous visit."

"Yeah, are you gonna be okay?"

"Fine, sir. Thank you for the washcloth." In fact, Jenny had nearly fainted on the spot when she burst into the suite and took in the sight: Sheldon and Alex, hastily dressed, and the king, breathing fire. The king had taken pity on her, made her sit down, and put a damp cloth on her forehead, which she had only given back in the last minute.

"How about your date? What happened to him?"

"My king, when I got the emergency call—I mean, when I was made aware of the occasion of your happy visit, he drove me back to the hotel and went home."

"Okay. Well, now that I'm sure we're not going to lose you, let me repeat, you're killin' me. You're not watching out for her?"

"Sir, she is her father's daughter."

"So?"

"So," Alex interrupted, "pull the other one, Dad. Why are you here? It's . . ." Alex glanced around for a clock.

"Eleven fifty-five," Jenny supplied helpfully.

"I haven't been getting any reports from you."

Alex looked at Jenny, who went redder, if possible (which perfectly matched her bloodshot eyes) and said, pretty much without taking a breath, "With all due respect sir and miss that's not true I've been filing reports at oh-eight-hundred and twenty-hundred hours each day."

"From *you*, sunshine," the king said to Alex. "Think I care what ribbon you cut or what jerk you had lunch with? I've got official reports coming out the yin-yang. This . . . *this* is the stuff I want to know about."

"*This* is none of your damned business."

"Guess again, Princess In-So-Much-Trouble. You, how about you?"

"Me?" Shel practically gulped. He was having trouble figuring out what was happening, and if a beating was imminent. Bad enough to be busted by a girl's dad . . . but a king? And now they were drinking decaf coffee in the suite's parlor, all of them sitting around the table like pals? Was death imminent? Deportation? Firing? Arm wrestling? What?

"Yeah, what's your story?"

Jenny leaned forward. "Dr. Sheldon Rivers, head of the—"

"Hush, Jenny," the king said, pleasantly enough, and she instantly hushed and stared down at her hands.

"Well, I'm—uh—I work at the Institute. I met your daughter her first day here and we've been . . ." He coughed. He had three cups of coffee in him; why was his mouth so dry? "We've been seeing each other."

"Seeing?" the king asked.

"Seeing?" Alex smirked, which was no help at all.

Shel felt his temper start to fray; it was like a rope being yanked along the top of a glass wall. "She's right," he said, almost snapped. "It's none of your business."

"Yeah, yeah." The king dipped a finger into his breast pocket and took out a small string that looked like an eight-inch length of dental floss. He started cleaning his teeth with it.

It *was* dental floss.

"Oh, Dad!" Alex cried, shielding her eyes from the horror. "Do you have to do that now?"

"Hey, I had a T-bone for supper. It's been driving me crazy." The floss twanged as he cleaned his incisors. "So, kiddo, when are you coming back?"

"I haven't decided yet."

This was news to Shel, who thought that perhaps the evening might be salvaged after all.

The king grunted. "Yeah?"

"Yeah."

"What if I told you to come back on the plane with me tomorrow morning, that David's finished up his projects and can take over for you here?" *Twang, pa-tang!*

"I'd tell you," she said cheerfully, "to take a flying fuck at a rolling donut."

"This is how she talks to her father," the king complained to Shel and Jenny. "Nice language."

"Who do you think I picked it up from?"

"I assumed TV, like everyone else."

"Maybe we should go," Shel said to Jenny.

"No," the king and princess said in unison.

"Kiddo, is this the way to go about fixing things?" the king continued, tucking his floss back in his pocket.

"You're not even going to throw it away?" Alex gasped.

"Waste not, want not."

"Dad, you're the *king* of *Alaska*. You can afford to use a new piece of dental floss now and again. My God, I'll buy you a new pack. A case. A factory. Just please, please throw that disgusting thing in the garbage."

"Hey, this way it's right here when I need it again." He patted his pocket.

She groaned into her palms, then looked back up at her father. "Every time I think I've figured out your disgusting habits, you come up with a new one."

"And you're avoiding the question. This the way to solve things?"

"What *things*, Dad?" she asked, exasperated.

"The insomnia-bad-dream-scared-all-the-time-things," Shel volunteered.

He got a double blast of Baranov blue—a glare from Alex; a look of surprise from the king.

"Never mind," Alex said.

"Huh," Al said.

"Never *mind*."

"So, boy, you're a doctor? Bio guy like my son?"

"Yes, sir."

"Don't call me sir, I work for a living."

"Dad! What's he supposed to say, 'hey schmuck'?"

"Army brat?" the king continued, pretending he wasn't being repeatedly interrupted.

"I'm sure it's in all your reports."

"Yeah, but who reads 'em? So, whaddya think of my kid here?"

"Daaaaaaaaaaad!"

"I think she's glorious," he said with perfect truth.

"Yeah? Huh." The king belched lightly against the back of his hand. "Plane food. It's always bad. Even if you own the plane. You free for dinner tomorrow night?"

"No," Alex said.

"Yes," Shel replied.

"You ever have dinner with a rich asshole before?"

"Sure," he said, and then he found out where Alex got the laugh.

Chapter 29

"**Y**our fish okay? Need another drink?"

"My fish is fine, King Alexander, and I need about five more drinks."

The king smiled. "I hear you. And it's Al."

"Dad, for God's sake," Alexandria broke in. "He's not going to call you Al. It's absurd."

"She's right," Shel agreed. "I'm not."

"What?" The king sounded wounded. "I'm trying to be nice. I'm all friendly and stuff. We're having a nice meal. I'm not putting him in crutches. I didn't declare war on his country. Why're you still bitching?"

"You wouldn't dare," Sheldon almost sneered. "America could kick your ass."

"Is that a *dare*, boy?"

"Stop it! Cut it out, you two, my God, it's like watching a couple of wolves in the backyard at home."

"Yeah, and there's only one alpha," King Al warned him.

"I was just thinking the same thing," Shel said mildly.

"Cut it out! I'm choking on all the testosterone in the air,

I swear. What are you looking at?" she snapped, and all the guards at the next table hurriedly looked elsewhere.

"Don't take your mad out on the staff," her father said in a tone that brooked no argument.

"Sorry," she said, and meant it. It had been one of the rules since earliest childhood: always smile, never fob the job on someone else, Edmund is always right, and never take a bad day out on the staff. "Okay, sorry. Sorry, guys," she called. Then she turned back to the two men in her life. "But Dad, honestly. 'Don't call me Sir, I'm Al' . . . give me a break. Do you think Prince Charles goes around saying 'hey, call me Chuck, how's it hangin'?' How about Princess Sophia of Greece? Do you think she says, 'call me Sophie, how 'bout some more salt on your grouper?' No."

"Aw, shaddup and eat your sushi."

She pursed her lips, then did as he commanded. Frankly, as far as dinners with a lover and her father went, the evening was, so far, a smashing success. Shel looked like he was about to jump out a window, but who could blame him? As if eating with her dad wasn't bad enough, there were six armed men at the next table.

"So, boy, what made you decide to be a marine biologist?"

"It's Shel. And I love the ocean."

"And you live here in NoDak?"

"Yes."

There was a long pause, but Shel didn't elaborate. The king tried again. "So, you ever been married?"

"You know I haven't, King Alexander."

"Well, it's overrated."

"Dad," Alex said warningly.

"Hey, I'm not saying she was a bad mom. Just a bad wife."

"Dad!"

"Man, the temper on her! Oofta. Reminds me of someone else," he said, glancing at Alex out of the corner of his eye.

"I read some stories about her."

"Oh, yeah?" the king asked warningly. The scandal surrounding Queen Dara's death had only been matched by the baying of the media dogs.

"Yeah. Something about on her way to her hairdresser's?"

It had actually been on the way to her lover's beach house, but the Sitka Palace, of course, had told a different story. In Alaska, it was very bad form to discuss the truth as opposed to the glossed-over press release.

The king relaxed. "Yeah. Damn shame, too. She was a beautiful woman. Sure didn't need any help from a hairdresser."

"Dad. Shel. Can we talk about something else, please?"

"Like what?" the king asked, clearly exasperated.

"Anything. God, anything! The melting ice caps. The rising American crime rate. Porn. We could talk about porn!"

"I'm not talking about porn with your dad," Shel informed her. "Not even if you stick a gun in my ear."

"Is that a dare, boy? Hey, Krenklov! Gimme your Sig."

"It's not a dare, Dad! You just put that right back in your holster, Terry."

"Spoilsport. You guys don't know from porn," the king said, and finished his beer. "Modern conveniences make porn a totally different undertaking."

Alex rested her head on her hands. "God, God . . ."

"Internet porn. Ha! You young men have it easy these days. When I was a kid, you got your porn the old-fashioned way: you sent your butler out to buy it, and you hid it where your mom's maid couldn't find it."

"Great," she sighed. "Just when I thought the evening couldn't get any weirder."

"Yeah," Shel agreed. "That was kind of naïve of you."

"Cheer up," the king told them. "Only three courses to go."

Chapter 30

Teal Grange parked his truck, which was so dusty it looked gray instead of yellow, and walked into the Pick n' Pin. He went straight to the bar to get a cup of beer, and instantly noticed all the men were sitting the wrong way. They had swiveled around on their stools and were watching the lanes. Which the bar guys never did.

Teal took his cup, then glanced over his shoulder to see what they were all staring at. And nearly dropped his cup on the popcorn-spotted carpet.

There was Jenny, ultra-yummy, petite, too-starched Jenny (he didn't know how she managed to look stiff in jeans, but she pulled it off). Jenny, marching over to the ball rack, grabbing one down, lugging it to her place at the foot of the lane, hurling it down the lane, waiting impatiently for a couple of pins to fall down, marching to the scoreboard and scribbling, then marching back to the ball rack.

"Wow!" he said, instantly dazzled. He glanced up at her score. Nothing to write home about, but a shitload better than the other night.

"Not only that," the bartender, Carol, said. She flung the bar cloth over one shoulder, grimaced, then pulled it off and tossed it in the sink. "She's been in here since we opened at nine. That's her—what? Twelfth game?"

"Fourteenth," the bar guys corrected her in dreamy unison.

"You're telling me she's been in here bowling all day?" He checked his watch. No, he wasn't late. "Jeez, it's almost suppertime."

"Yeah, getting a little good at it, too," one of the bar guys said. "Christ, look at those legs. Black denim, ah-yup."

"I like 'em taller," another bar guy said.

"When they look like that, I don't care if they're a fucking midget."

"Don, you wouldn't care if they were a cat."

"She should pull her hair out of that ponytail. I bet it'd look good on my pillow," another bar guy joked.

"Shut up about that," Teal ordered. "Stop speculating about my . . . date."

Yeah, date. That was about it. Jenny wasn't in town long, for one thing. For another, she was already married to her job. For another, though he'd sell his soul for a shot at her in the sack, she clearly had no ambition to see *him* naked.

He was there strictly for entertainment value. Someone for her to talk to during the rare moments she wasn't working. Frankly, he was amazed they'd made it past the first date. Zero in common, *nada*, zilch. But ooh, those eyes . . . and he didn't mind them short. At five nine, he was in no position to be picky about height.

Still, it wasn't every day a good-looking brunette wanted to bowl with him, and he definitely took what he could get.

"I see any more leers tonight, I'm pulling tongues out and wiping the bar with them," he warned.

"Great!" Carol said. "When do you think you'll get on that?"

He sighed. "Gimme a bottle of water, please."

He took his beer and the water over to Jenny, who had just hurled a split.

"Damn! You're getting good at this!"

"I've been practicing. Thank you." She accepted the water, and glugged it thirstily. "The Princess gave me the day off, so I left a message for you and came here."

"Jeez, that was, like, ages ago. I'm sorry, I had to take out a bunch of tourists, I didn't even have my signal until a little while ago."

"It's fine. Wretched ball," she muttered, plucking it off the roller and marching to the line.

"Is that what you say to psych yourself up?"

"No." She hurled again with a gasp, knocking over the fourth, seventh, and eighth pins. "Dammit!"

He sipped his beer and sat down at the scoring machine. She puffed a strand of hair off her sweaty forehead and waited for her ball to come back.

"So," he began carefully, thinking that the bowling balls might as well be mines. *Might as well get to it. Please God, don't let her throw one of the damn things at me.* "How'd it go after I dropped you off?"

"Oh, fine. Just . . . family business."

"You get in trouble?"

"The Princess protects me from that. Not many would, you know. Many who work for royalty are used to—" She cut herself off. "I'm sorry. I'm tired and upset, and I'm saying too much."

"Well, shit, you wanna go back to the hotel? I mean, you've been at this for a while."

"No, I don't want to go back there. If I go back there I'll want to work. And right now, for the first time in my life, I do *not* want to work."

"You—you don't?" He was almost afraid to ask. "Then, uh, whaddya want to do?"

She looked at him and for the second time in five minutes, he almost dropped his beer. Gone was the skittering gaze of the shy woman he'd been getting to know; this was a woman who knew *exactly* what she was after, and full speed ahead. He was almost afraid of this one.

"I'd like to see where you live."

He stared. And stared. And stared some more. Finally, to be sure, he said, "Where I live? As in, where I sleep? Where my bed is?"

"Yes." She ignored her ball when it came spinning back to her. Her gaze was like a laser. "Where your bed is."

"Well . . . okey-dokey. Do you want to get something to eat fir—"

"No."

"Because we don't have to get a burger, we could stop somewhere and get a sal—"

"No."

"I guess," he said, totally mystified, "we'd better go, then."

"Very good, Teal."

Chapter 31

Teal pulled up outside a charming bank of sky-colored condos, got out of his filthy truck, walked around, and opened her door. "Mine's the one on the end," he said. "Sixteen hundred sixty six."

"The mark of the beast," she said gravely.

"Yeah, watch out for the elevator full of blood. That can be such a drag sometimes."

She might have laughed, but she was too nervous. She was a bundle of nerves, in fact, and all that energy had to go somewhere. Why not into Teal? He was a nice enough fellow. He looked fabulous. He looked *incredible*. His jeans were filled out in the most wonderful way, and so was his rust-colored work shirt. She'd have to do something about the ponytail, though. But the hair—dirty blond, streaked by the sun—was wonderful, thick, like living gold. The glasses made him look thoughtful and smart.

And the eyes . . . the color of the Caribbean, the color of spring. She'd never seen such green eyes before. It was difficult to look away from them, and she'd spent a lifetime getting used to Baranov blue.

She followed him up the steps to his front door, still

silently fuming about the events of the night before. She knew the Princess was a grown woman, that she herself was faultless, but she resented the king's implication that she hadn't done her job.

He was just upset, she reminded herself for the thousandth time. You're reading far too much into it.

Still. It hurt like nothing else had, except the death of her father. The king's disapproval. And where had she been on the night in question? Busy with paperwork? No indeed. She'd been *bowling*. Which, to make everything much worse, she was *bad* at.

Well, there was one thing she could control—two, actually—and getting better at that silly game was big number one on the list.

"Here we are," said big number two, swinging the door open for her. She walked past him, taking in a surprisingly neat abode for a man who lived alone. "So, you want a beer? A shot?"

She had a glimpse of piles and piles of laundry before he kicked the door shut. "Guest room," he explained with a cough. "Not that I have any. Well, actually, I will. My brother's coming tonight to crash for a couple of days."

"Crane, Robin, Crow, or Raven?"

He looked pleased. "Hey, you remembered! You listen real good."

"It's my job." She added through gritted teeth, "Which I'm *very very very* good at."

"Whoa. Okay, calm down. And sit down." He led her to the couch. "I know you're not the boozing type, but I really think you need a drink."

"Very well. And you didn't answer my question," she called after him as he disappeared into the kitchen.

"Crane. Robin and Raven are my sisters. Anyway, I didn't think you'd—I mean, when I told him he could crash here I honestly never thought you'd even see my—anyway, he's coming tonight."

"I won't stay long, then," she said,

"No no no. I mean, stay as long as you want. I don't give a shit." He held out a small glass half filled with yellowish-brown liquid.

"Cognac?" she asked, sniffing doubtfully.

"Jack Daniel's. Drink up."

She did, and instantly assumed the action was going to kill her. It seemed as if her lungs, trachea, and stomach were all trying to leap out onto Teal's dun-colored carpet at once.

"Feel better?" he asked solicitously, downing his own drink and smacking his lips.

"Loads," she gasped, putting the glass down on the newspapers with fingers that trembled. That was when she noticed . . . "How many copies of the paper did you buy?"

"Well, all my sibs wanted a copy. And my folks. And I bought one for his mom, because God knows *he* won't think of it. He's real insensitive like that," Teal confided, plopping down on the couch beside her.

"Men can be that way," she said darkly.

"Ah-ha! So it's the king you're pissed at, not Alex."

"I'm just . . . tired. I'm ready to go back home. I really want to get back home." She realized how grumpy and inappropriate that sounded and hastily regrouped. "Not that it isn't a lovely state, but I just—I—"

"You want another drink?" he asked, green eyes anxious.

"No! I mean, no thank you. I want . . . you."

"What? Ow! Hey, that's my last clean shirt. Be careful with—" Then he wasn't talking anymore, lord be praised, because she had seized him with her tiny fists, her lust and anger giving her the strength of the gods. She pulled him close to her and mashed her lips on his for a good long time.

"Please let me go," he gasped after a minute.

"Take me into your bedroom," she growled.

"Seriously, I've got some mace around here I think . . . I got it for my sister's birthday, but that's not 'til next month . . ."

"Make love to me."

"But . . . okay. No, wait! Look, you're great and all, but you know the same thing as me."

"What? Nevermind. Less talking," she ordered. "More undressing."

He was trying to gently fend her off with an elbow as she rained kisses on his neck. "Ack! That tickles. Look, Jenn, I think you're cool and all—well, a little starchy, maybe—but you don't want to do this. You really don't."

"Yes I do. Do you have condoms?"

"Yes I do. Wait a minute! Aren't you listening to a damn word? We don't have a thing in common. If I was in Alaska, you'd never have given me a second look."

"That's not true," she muttered into his neck. "I think you're extremely attractive and annoyingly sexy."

"Well, yeah, there's definitely a chemistry thing going on here, but that's all. You'll be really mad at yourself in the morning."

"A pleasant change from being mad at—at things out of my control."

"Ah-ha!"

"Stop saying that. What's wrong with your belt? It's like there's a combination lock on it."

"Look, just . . . stop that . . ." He grabbed her hands and forced them into her lap. "Just . . . calm down now and stop getting me all worked up. I mean, I'm a nice fuckin' guy but only for so long."

"Too long," she grumped.

"Just, take a breath, okay? Relax. Caaaaaalm down. You're having a shitty day—week, maybe—and that happens to everybody."

"That has nothing to do with anything."

"No, no, it's okay! Shit, just the other day, some dildo-brain was all, 'I can't find the bail on my reel' and nearly poked my eye—never mind, it's boring. Anyway, my point is, you shouldn't do something you'll regret the shit out of later, just because the king hurt your feelings."

"He didn't mean it," she said automatically. "He was upset."

"Well, yeah! Believe me, I got the whole yuck-o story from Shel this morning."

"You did?" She didn't know if that was horrifying, or a relief. Of course, Dr. Rivers wasn't under the same constraints as she was. He wasn't staff, he was . . . something else.

"Oh, yeah! The king! Coming out of nowhere like Batman! Busted in on them! Practically naked! Shel and Alex, I mean. Then he freaks out and practically has Shel shot on the spot. *Then* he takes 'em out for dinner—I dunno which is worse."

"Thanks for the recap," she said dryly, "but I was there."

"It's no wonder everybody's upset. The way I hear it, that guy fills up every room he's ever in. I can't think of a better way to squash a, what d'you call it, a budding romance."

"Is that what it is?" she asked, immediately alert. "Because the princess doesn't . . . I mean, she has had no long-term involvements. Ever." That was safe enough. Anyone who had read *People* magazine knew that much.

"Trust me: they're going to get married. I have *never* seen Shel this rattled. He's overlooked all his prejudices to be with her. Next thing, he'll be eating cheese."

"He—the king—he implied that I—that I had not been doing my job."

Teal laughed so hard he almost fell off the couch. Jenny stared at him coldly. "I fail to see the humor you've found."

"Do you hear yourself, woman? Nobody with half a brain could ever think that, not in a million years of thinking. You have no life! Everybody knows that!"

She cheered up a little. "Really?"

"Honey, you're pathetic! You didn't even bring blue jeans . . . to North Dakota! The princess had to *order* you to actually leave the hotel to even go on a date."

She cheered up more. "That's true."

"It's so fuckin' stupid that you've got this idea in your head that *anybody* thinks you're doing a bad job, much less King Hot Shit."

"Mr. Grange!"

"See? You can't even be mad at him properly. You suck at that, too! And you *really* suck at being bad at your job."

She smiled a little. "You're just saying that to cheer me up."

"No, Jenn, I swear! You're the biggest workaholic loser I've ever seen."

She rested her head on his shoulder. "You're very sweet."

"And weird, did I mention weird? Because if I said all that shit to any other girl on the planet, she'd kick me in the nuts."

"No, the time for foreplay has passed," she sighed. She straightened up, patted her hair, and made sure her shirt was tucked in. "You're right, it would have been an error of grotesque proportions."

"Jeez, I didn't exactly put it like—"

She took one of his blocky hands in hers and squeezed. "Thank you for not taking advantage of me, Teal. I'll always be grateful. I never would have forgiven myself for doing something so impulsively unwise."

"Uh, you're welcome."

"You were so sweet to listen to my problems and help me understand them a little better."

"I'm an asshole," he grumped. "Golden opportunity to get laid by a hottie and I talk her out of it."

"Yes, you did," she said happily, standing. "And you've earned my eternal devotion and friendship."

"Great. That and a fuckin' dollar, I can buy a Coke."

"I'll buy you all the Cokes you want," she promised. "But first you must take me back to the hotel."

"Welcome back, non-bowling workaholic loser."

"It's good to be me," she said, completely seriously.

Chapter 32

"Come," the king called.

The knock on the door, quick and firm, came again.

"Come on *in*," the king called, louder.

Wham! Wham! Wham!

"Jesus!" the king screamed. "Come in, for Christ's sake!"

"Come," Alex said, and the door opened. "Hi, Shel."

"That's gonna get real fuckin' old real quick," the king said.

"It's *her* room," Shel retorted. He walked in, slung his pack on an empty chair—to Alex's extreme relief, it didn't clink—and sat down beside Alex on the small couch. Her father was sprawled behind one of the desks, doing another of his dratted puzzles . . . the crossword, this time. "So, am I interrupting anything?"

"Naw," Al replied. "We're just talking about some upcoming stuff. Weddings and shit. What's a four-letter word for to hit or push against?"

"Butt," Shel said.

"Hmmm." He scribbled it down. "So, you two going out tonight, or what?"

"We usually stay in," Alex said smoothly. "Order room service, watch a movie."

"Sounds like plenty."

"How long are *you* staying?" Shel asked pointedly.

Her father gave him a look she knew well. "Dunno. I just got here. It's real pretty here. I might stay a while. Now quit buggin' me, I gotta think. Four letter word," he mused aloud, "for advance."

"Come," Sheldon said.

Alex chewed on her lower lip so she wouldn't burst into hysterical giggles. Shel shot her a look and she could see by the way his eyes were watering that he was having trouble swallowing his own laughter.

"You okay?" the king asked. "You look a little constipated."

"I'm fine, King Al."

"Hump!"

"What, Dad?"

"A rounded mass, i.e., the structure on the back of a camel. Hump. Damn, I've just about got this thing licked. Next time I'm doing it in pen." He looked up at Shel. "I'm pretty fuckin' smart, you know."

"Yes, King Al."

"No, really. I mean, we don't all have hotshot PhDs but that doesn't mean we're stupid."

"Dad, please." Alex tried to mask her exasperation. Although her father had insisted all his children get at least a four-year degree, he himself had never indulged. So his attitude toward those with degrees was mixed: admiration and envy. Good work, but don't let it go to your head. "Everybody knows you're smart. Almost as smart as me, even."

"Har, har."

There was a discreet rap at the door, which opened at Al's absent, "Come!"

Edmund, the king's right hand man, entered after a polite pause. Alex could see Shel gaping at him, which was perfectly understandable. Her sister called him Ichabod Brain. Tall as the king, but much thinner, he looked as though he'd be at home in the starched suits and powdered wigs of two hundred years ago. As it was, he looked plenty starched in the severe gray suit and highly polished black shoes.

"Hey, Eds, what's a nine-letter word for creating an obstacle?"

"L-O-O-K-I-T-U-P."

"Har fucking har."

Edmund bowed. "Your Majesty. Your Highness. Dr. Rivers."

"Uh, hi," Shel said.

"Don't freak," Alex said. "He knows everybody's name."

"That's true, Your Highness." He stepped up to the desk. "I've brought some correspondence, my king, but the thing you desire most has not shown up."

"The ring of Sauron?" Alex guessed.

"Oh, like I couldn't have about ten of those made if I wanted. No, I'm waiting for the invite. We better figure out which one of us is going to go."

"Where?" Alex asked.

"William's wedding."

"*Prince* William? From England?" Shel shook his head, which Alex found understandable. Her father talked about the Windsors like they were neighbors. In fact, he had a charming blind spot about Queen Elizabeth, the matriarch, which prevented him from—

"So, which one of us is going? Alex? You want to? Maybe I should, though. Head of the family and all. But Charles and Christina really hit it off at her wedding, maybe I should send her and David."

"Um, Dad, have you thought—have you considered—" She looked up; Edmund's eyes were pleading with her. The coward! He hadn't brought up the possibility. Once again, it was up to her to save the family honor. Nuts! "Maybe the queen won't be sending us an invitation."

Her father looked honestly puzzled. "What? Why?"

"Well . . . because she hates you and thinks you're a boorish clown."

"Oh, that." He waved away with one blocky hand his attempted murder of the queen's favorite corgi. "We got that straightened out when I was in the hospital."

"When you tried to seduce her."

"Hey, she likes me!"

"You tried to have sex with the queen of—"

"Quiet, boy. You really don't think she'll invite us? How can she not invite us? I've known her my whole life!"

"Perhaps," Edmund suggested, "that is part of the problem."

"You don't think she's mad because we didn't invite her to Dara's christening, do you?" he asked anxiously. "Because that was just family and *really* close friends. There were only about forty people there. She wouldn't take that personal, right?"

"I'm certain not, Your Majesty."

"No," Alex agreed, "that's definitely not it."

"I was at *her* wedding, *and* Charles's, and you're saying she won't invite me to the kid's? Fucking Joan Rivers is going, but not me? Not that I think he should be getting married," he added in a mutter, "not at his age."

"Dad, he's almost as old as I am."

"Tell me. Kid should run around a little more; trust me, the girls will wait."

"Perhaps the mail has been delayed," Edmund said. "It has to come from England, after all, and then be routed to the States."

King Alexander visibly perked up. "Sure, that's what it is."

Alex glared at Edmund, who was only making it worse. Getting the man's hopes up! Queen Elizabeth wouldn't invite her father if it meant getting Ireland back. "She'd probably invite you," Alex said, "if she knew you wouldn't come."

"Well, somebody has to go."

"No, really. Dad. I don't think she'd mind if the Baranov family skipped a Windsor wedding."

"It's kind of mean."

"She'll understand."

"Well, I'll think about it."

"That's all I'm saying." Then, "Edmund," she asked sweetly, "may I see you in the other room for a moment?"

"Now just a minute," her father said. "It was all me, kiddo. He didn't do anything."

"You lie," she told the monarch, "like old people fuck."

"I am, of course, at Her Highness's disposal."

"Good. Hallway. Now."

"You're not *leaving* me with him?" Shel asked, horrified, just as she stepped into the hall with Edmund and pulled the door shut.

"What can I do for you, Prin—"

"Edmund, you suck!"

"Tone, Princess. 'A member of the royal family must always—'"

"*How* could you bring him here, how, *how?* Are you *trying* to ruin my life?"

"No," he admitted, "it just happens on its own, sometimes."

"You got me to come out here, no doubt some loser plan you and Dr. Pohl cooked up, then you showed him the *Minot Daily News*—"

"The king likes to keep up with current events."

"Oh, bullshit! He never would have seen that if you hadn't stuck it under his nose, not with all the junk he has to wade through every day, and sure as shit not when it's fishing season. So did you send me out here to have a good time, or not?"

"I confess," he confessed, "the picture startled me. I—we—were concerned you were perhaps . . . confused. Possibly from lack of sleep."

"That's very flattering, Edmund, you—you—" She couldn't do it. He was *staff*, he worked for *them*, but she could no more insult him, fire him, smack him, then she could drench her hair with gasoline and light a match. "I'm not confused! Okay, I am. But bringing my dad—my *dad!*—out here is not helping."

"Perhaps you will come to a decision about Dr. Rivers."

"Perhaps I've only known him a week! We can't *date*, you never heard of dating? What, I've got to drop him or marry him? There's nothing in the middle? What is this, an episode of *Beat the Clock?*"

"Princess, you don't date. Quite frankly, until I saw that picture, I had assumed you were still . . . ah . . . never mind."

She buried her fists in her hair and fought the urge to pull out heavy chunks. "God . . . God . . . I'm not telling you when I lost my virginity, that's for damned sure."

"Thank heavens."

"In fact, we're not having this conversation at all."

"Also good, Your Highness."

She stuck a finger under his nose. He raised his brows at her, but didn't flinch. She practically had to stretch to *reach* his nose, which made it difficult to exude authority. "For the record, buster, I'm *very* disappointed in you. I could have been spared that whole scene the other night if you weren't such a fucking meddler."

"Language, Princess."

"Stop it! What I do—or don't do—or do—with Dr. Rivers is my own business. Not yours, not the king's. Got it?"

"Yes, Princess."

"I know you're the king's man, just like Jenny's first loyalty is to me, but—"

"Ah, Jenny," Edmund mused, staring into space. "I must speak to her. She's managed to avoid me thus far."

"Don't you say a damned word to her! And you can consider that a *royal command*. Got it?"

"Yes, Princess."

It worked! She'd never given a royal command before. But the situation was dire. To put it mildly. "All right. We're done."

"May I take my leave, Your Highness?"

"You can take a long walk off a short pier for all I care."

"Tone, Princess. And good night."

Chapter 33

"Finally," she groaned, flopping down on the bed. "I didn't think they'd ever leave."

"*You* didn't think?" Sheldon was slumped in the chair in the corner. Her father had left typical chaos in his wake—papers, invitations, crossword puzzles, word finds. She had gladly shut the door on the mess, and led Shel to the bedroom. "You should have seen me and your dad trying to pretend like we couldn't hear you ripping Ed a new one. Awkward."

"Never Ed. Edmund." Then she realized what he had said. "You could?" She was instantly appalled. "You heard the whole thing?"

"No, just when you screamed," he said matter-of-factly. "A royal command, eh? Does that actually work?"

"We'll find out. Maybe I'll give you one."

"Sorry, sunshine. American citizen."

"Mmph." She studied her bare toes for a moment, then said, "It's so hard to yell at him. It's like yelling at my dad. I mean, I can do it, but it's tricky."

"Grew up with him?"

"Oh, yes. In fact, I saw much more of him than my mother."

"Yeah, but if he gets really out of line you could just . . . you know. Fire him."

"No I can't."

"Sure you can. I mean, end of the day, he's just another employee, right?"

She had the impression he was baiting her. Testing her. Which she had no interest in, or time for. "No," she said coldly, "and don't talk about him like that."

"Sorry," he said, not sounding sorry at all. "You wouldn't do that, huh?"

"Shel, having people work for you isn't quite the song-and-dance you think it is. And when you're us—the people who work for you, they do it for generations. They're like family. I know it's a cliché, but it's true. I'd never fire Edmund, I'd never fire Jenny. Her mom worked for my mom, you know? I played with her when we were kids."

"So you've never fired anybody at your castle?"

"Well, of course, we—Sheldon. Are we going to fight, or fuck?"

"Can't we do both?"

"Well, I'd rather do the latter, but if you want to pick a fight—"

"Okay, okay. You're pissy, I'm pissy . . . we're stressed out because your dad's here."

"To put it mildly," she admitted.

"God, that scene! And then dinner last night!" He slapped his forehead. "I don't know which was worse. And can you imagine if he'd showed up half an hour earlier? Jesus! My dick wants to fall off just thinking about it."

"If you ever want to have sex with me again, we'll *stop* talking about it."

"Done and done."

She watched as he got up and went to his backpack. "Are you hungry?"

"Only for depraved lovemaking. Whoops, sorry. I meant sex."

She giggled. "Depraved? Is that what it is?"

He pulled out a wad of cloth, brought it to the bed, and separated it. She realized the wad was neckties. Four of them.

"Genius," she said approvingly. "I'm so glad your bag didn't clink while my dad was here."

"Not fucking likely, no pun intended. Besides, I half thought he was going to have me strip-searched. The last thing I wanted him to find was our toys. Ties, I could try to explain."

She laughed again. "Depraved . . . is that the word of the day? Like I said, I haven't thought of it like that. I've just been enjoying it. You know?"

"You have to admit," he said, smoothing out the ties, "most people start with vanilla and work their way up to kink."

"Yes, I have to admit that. Bring those over here." After a minute, she said, "Ugh."

"Hey, not everybody can afford silk, Princess."

"Don't start."

Chapter 34

Jenny triple-checked the next day's itinerary. With the king in town, everything had gotten exponentially more complicated, and that was just the security detail. Fortunately, Edmund was in charge of finding amusing puzzles for the king; she just had to worry about scheduling.

But things looked good. Even better, she was in her favorite suit, a cranberry Anne Klein, with sheer black hose and sensible dark pumps. Jeans were just . . . weird.

Her cell phone buzzed, and she picked it up, expecting to hear an all's well night check from one of the guards. "Yes?"

"Jenn? It's Teal."

"Oh . . . hello." She nearly blushed when she remembered her actions earlier. It was apparently catching . . . wearing denim, seducing travel guides, the princess seeing someone, the king showing up unannounced . . . insanity! "What can I do for you, Teal?"

She had a horrible thought: he'd changed his mind! He wanted her to spend the night! And it would only be her fault, for giving him the wrong idea in the first place. Throwing herself at him like that. She shivered just thinking about it.

"Jenn? Hello? You still there?"

"Yes, I—I'm sorry. Go ahead. How can I help you?"

"Well, my brother's here, and if you're not too busy, I thought I'd bring him over to the hotel to meet you." He lowered his voice. "He's dying to meet you."

Relief flooded her like sweet wine. His brother! A social call! That she could handle. The week she'd been having, it was probably the only thing she could handle.

She checked her watch. Nine-thirty. Alex had bid her goodnight some time ago. Dr. Rivers would spend the night, or not, but either way, that door wouldn't open for at least three hours. And she *was* caught up on her paperwork. And she'd been technically off duty for almost an hour . . . "Are you sure? It's a little late for you, isn't it?"

"Don't sweat it, Mom."

"Hush up. What I meant is, don't you have an early group tomorrow?"

"No, I blew those dumbasses off. My bro's here, so we're gonna do the town."

"Oh. Well, come on over, then. I'll make sure security lets you up. I'm looking forward to meeting your brother."

"I don't know why," Teal grumped. "He's a dick."

She laughed. Then she added, because it had happened to her many times before, "But you might tell him that the princess isn't receiving visitors until nine o'clock tomorrow."

"It's not like that, Jenn. He wants to meet *you*. Don't ask me why. Well, if you did ask, I might 'fess up to how I rhapsodized about how your butt looks in brand-new Levi's."

She rolled her eyes. "How can you use 'dumbasses' and 'rhapsodizes' in the same conversation?"

"It's a gift, bay-bee. See in you twenty."

A nice man, she thought, filing paperwork into overnight satchels. *Coarse, but nice . . . he didn't take advantage of my moment of weakness, so who cares how often he says 'dumbass'?*

It's just too bad we don't have more in common. Anything in common. She paused wistfully, staring off into space. *There must be someone out there who wouldn't resent my long hours, my devotion to the family . . . someone who—*

She cut off the nonsense—in fact, there wasn't, and there was no use crying about it—and notified Security that there would be visitors.

Chapter 35

She strained against the neckties, to no avail, of course—Dr. Rivers must have been a boy scout, or a sailor, because he could tie a helluva knot.

Right now the boy scout was licking the underside of her breast with careful attention, such careful attention that she thought she was going to go crazy. They'd been at it for hours, it seemed, she was more than ready for him, and still all he did was kiss and nibble and suck and lick and stroke, no matter how much she begged him, pleaded, ordered, demanded. She'd finally quit when he pleasantly informed her he was sure he could find something in the room that could be used as a gag.

Now he was kissing her mouth and she opened for him like his mouth was made of honey, and at the same time she felt his fingers slide into her, stroking her slick wetness, just barely coming into her, then withdrawing. Teasing, stroking, dipping. She strained against him, against her bonds, trying to force more of him into her, and he laughed into her mouth.

"What do you think the king would say if I planted a big hickey on your throat?" he asked.

"I don't care," she groaned. "Please fuck me now, before I have a heart attack."

"I think you're safe," he replied. "If anyone in this room is in danger of an M.I., it's me. My God, you're so lush . . . you're like a banquet." He pulled back and looked at her nude, spread-eagle body with unconcealed admiration. "Right now I'm the luckiest guy on the whole planet."

He leaned down and cupped her other breast with one hand, sucking the swollen nipple into his mouth. She arched to meet him, knowing it wouldn't do any good, knowing she couldn't help it.

He worked his way down her writhing body, raining kisses on her and then flicking through her damp folds with his tongue.

He licked and kissed between her thighs for an excruciatingly lovely time, and she felt her middle clench, felt the familiar sensation of falling, and then she was crying out to the ceiling.

"I love that sound," he said, coming up to her, taking his cock in one hand and beginning to ease into her. "God, I love that sound."

"And I love . . ." *You. No. It's the moment.* Right? ". . . that. Oh, I love that. Wait. Stop."

He did, at once. "What's the matter?"

"Come up here. Bring that up here."

His eyes widened and then he grinned, a smile full of unrestrained lust, and climbed up, carefully settling his knees on either side of her head.

Her mouth opened and he eased past her teeth, already shuddering, and she sucked him all the way in, inhaling his scent, his dick, his everything.

"Oh jeeeeeeeeeeeeeeezus," he slurred, gently rocking back and forth. "Oh, God, you should be against the law. Oh God, your mouth . . . your mouth . . ."

She licked his salty tip, her tongue frantically padding

against him, enjoying the feel of him in her mouth—this was something new, this was delightful, knowing he could be rough with her and wasn't, knowing he could push himself all the way into her throat and she couldn't stop him. It made his care almost mind-bogglingly erotic. It made her suck as hard as she could. It made her—

Abruptly he jerked out, leaving her gasping. "Was I hurting you?" she groaned.

"Not hardly. About two more seconds of that," he panted, easing down her body, "and we'd be done."

"Perish the . . ." was as far as she got because he was filling her up, slowly and tenderly, as though she might break, as though he might

love you

care for her, and she whimpered as he pressed forward.

"Oh, God," she managed, and then couldn't talk, didn't want to talk as his tongue swept into her mouth, as he filled her up, stroked, thrust, sped up, as she came again and again, as he shivered over her, as he buried his face in her throat, as he whispered something she did not understand, on purpose.

Chapter 36

Security buzzed her and let Jenny know that Teal and his brother were coming up, so she went to stand by the elevator, exchanging a pleasant greeting with Krenklov on the way.

She smoothed her skirt and her hair, and when the elevator dinged and the doors started to wheeze open, she had a smile ready. A smile which instantly froze on her face.

"Hi, Jenn. This is my brother, Crane."

She said nothing.

Crane held out a manicured hand. The nails were neatly short, and buffed. She stared at it. "A great pleasure to meet you," he rumbled. "Teal's told me so many great things about you."

A short, difficult silence followed.

"Anyway," Teal said finally, giving her a strange look, "we thought we'd pop by, try to talk you into coming out for a beer. Not that you drink beer. Maybe a coffee? We can probably find a place that'll serve coffee without drowning it in whipped cream . . ."

"There's an excellent wine bar about six blocks from here," Crane said. "I had a 1944 Sauternes there."

Jenny's tongue felt frozen in her mouth.

"Of course, the port from that year was dreadful."

"You—"

Teal rolled his eyes. "I know, what a fucking stiff! 'Dreadful,' who says dreadful?"

"Someone with a more developed brain than you, little brother," Crane retorted.

"Shut the hell up. Jenn, are you going to shake his hand or is it going to just hang in the air all night?"

She shook the hand, which was strong and smooth at the same time. "I'm—I'm very pleased to meet you." She glanced over at his brother and hissed, "You didn't tell me you had an identical twin!"

Teal shrugged. "Why?"

"I'm afraid I'm a bit of the family black sheep," Crane said politely, staring at her with green, green eyes. "Everyone else works outdoors as trainers or guides or what-have-you. I rebelled a bit."

"Went fag is more like it," Teal said helpfully.

She took in the dark suit, the white shirt, the polished black shoes, the clean-shaven features. "Wh—what do you do?" she asked, staring up at him with helpless longing.

"I'm third violin for the Boston Symphony."

"Symphony," she breathed, swaying on her heels.

"Yes, well, I'm afraid I'm out here sulking, I missed my shot at second chair. My brother offered to cheer me up, and so here I am."

"That's great. I mean awful. Very very awful. You know, there's a symphony in Anchorage. And the king has wanted to get one started in Juneau. But it's difficult to get musicians to come all that way."

He smiled down at her. "Really? I can't think of a single reason not to go."

Ohhhhhhhhhhh . . .

"Beer? Wine? Tequila? Anything? You guys? Hello?"

"Do you know, you look extraordinarily like the ballerina Greta Hodgkinson?"

She gasped. "You know, I've always thought so!"

Chapter 37

"This place," Teal said, "is the worst. I mean, it blows. It blows rocks."

"Hush, Teal," Crane said, almost absently, staring raptly into Jenny's eyes.

"We had to drive almost two hours to get here? Jesus."

"Yes," Jenny said. "Hush."

"For Christ's sake," he grumped, reading the menu again, which still only had three entrees on it. Three! Any decent restaurant had pages and pages of menu you could flip through. "You can't even get a burger here!"

"Ohhh, how wonderful," Jenny breathed. "No burgers."

"But they have a lovely marbled strip steak, which they serve with the most cunning béarnaise sauce . . . I think it has a hint of chervil in it. It's nothing I've been able to put my finger on . . ."

"Oh, delicious," Jenny said. "I'd like to have that, please. Except on bread; skip the steak."

"And I *don't* want something that looks like the dog threw up on it before they brought it to my table," Teal griped. "Isn't anything in this place plain, for a working man? I mean, shee-it."

His twin and his friend looked at him with identical reproachful expressions, and Teal almost shuddered. Usually, his ideas were in the majority—Crane was definitely the black sheep of the family. And whatever friend they were hanging out with—like Shel, for instance—usually blew off the fancy sauces, especially if they were cheese-based.

Now, for the first time in his life, Crane was in the company of people who held the class-based high ground—and knew it. He felt like shriveling in his chair. Which pissed him off. Which made him feel like talking more.

"I mean, why fuck up a perfectly good piece of red meat? Why fancy it up with all that shit? Why not just throw it on the grill for ten minutes on each side and you're all set? Maybe with some mashed on the side . . ."

Jenny shivered and Crane patted her hand. "You can't overcook red meat, Teal. All the flavor will be lost. And the sauce works in concert with the full-bodied flavor of the meat. Assuming you even want red meat."

"Too true," Crane said, nodding, "and if you serve it with anything, it should be with something a little more delicate, in contrast to the robust texture of the meat."

"Like sautéed morel mushrooms," Jenny added. "Or, out of season, perhaps straw mushrooms. And perhaps some sautéed baby spinach on the side."

"That sounds heavenly," Crane breathed.

"Great. A serving of mold next to my pile of dog barf."

"Hush," they both murmured.

"Christ on a stick," Teal grumbled. The waiter edged over and—and! They talked about wine for. Ten. Minutes. Red wine, white wine, oaked wine, whatever the fuck that was. Ice wine, which wasn't appropriate until dessert, assuming he made it that long.

Finally . . . finally! Crane and Jenn had ordered their glasses, and the waiter was looking at him expectantly.

"Do you speak beer?" he asked him.

"Yes, of course," the waiter said, and Teal nearly swooned. "We have an excellent selection from Europe: Kolsch, Staro-proman, Warsteiner, Zipfer, and, of course, Hoegartner."

Teal whimpered.

"You might try the Zipfer," his brother suggested, the traitorous fuck. "You can drink quite a bit and it doesn't cause hangovers."

"Good," Teal snapped, "because I'm gonna drink a *lot*. Bring on the Zips," he told the waiter, who smiled and walked away.

"Ugh, beer," Jenny said, wrinkling her nose.

"It's just so . . ." His fag brother groped for the word.

"Common," Jenny prompted.

"Exactly. Now a solid, oaked white, on the other hand . . ."

"You could hardly call it common."

"When the wine comes," he informed Tweedle Dum and Tweedle Dummer, "I'm cutting the cork in half and sticking each piece in my ear. It's an alternative to slitting both your throats."

"Now you're just being a baby," Jenny said reproachfully. "You should be happy I find your brother so—ah—engag-ing."

"Not if it means I'm going to be bored out of my tits all night," he snapped back.

"I can't believe I almost . . ." She shut up and sipped from her water glass.

"Believe me, 'narrow escape' is the phrase that's been on my mind all evening, too." He gulped his water thirstily . . . where was the Zipper beer? He needed about ten.

"I'm delighted you find me engaging," his brother said, and Jenny blushed to her eyebrows. "And speaking of engag-ing, I don't think we should delay even a moment."

"Oh, I agree," Jenny said, blinking up at him with her big

Shania Twain eyes. "I think, if you find that person, that certain someone—I despise the term soul mate because it's—it's—"

"So dreadfully overused."

"Yes! But when you do find such a creature, someone so in sync, there seems no point to delay."

"I agree."

"I'm so happy to hear that!"

"Not as happy as I am, Jenny." They hugged briefly, and Teal barely rescued their water glasses.

"What the hell is this?" he asked.

They untangled each other, each beaming at him like pod people. "Congratulate us, dear," Jenny said.

"Congratulate you for *what?* Macking at the table in the most expensive restaurant in the state?"

"Yes, give us all your best wishes," his weirdo brother added, still holding Jenny's hand.

"You guys. Seriously. What the hell is going on?"

They stared deeply into each other's eyes, and Teal was about to repeat the question, louder, when they turned to him and said in unison, "We're engaged!"

In fact, you can get a hangover if you drink too many Zipfer beers.

Chapter 38

Alex was cuddled in Shel's arms and it was, at the moment, difficult to feel concerned about anything. Instead, she actually felt sleepy. Not the exhaustion of knowing she hadn't slept enough and wouldn't in the future, but actual "it's possible to doze off" sleepy.

"That was yummy," she sighed, stroking her fingers along his bicep.

"The yummiest in my life. We keep topping each other."

She laughed. "Is that supposed to be a joke?"

"No. Because if it was, it'd be a pretty bad one, don't you think?"

"Do you want me to call room service, have them send up a steak?"

"I'd be too tired to cut it."

"I could have someone cut it."

He groaned. "What a great way to shatter my post-coital bliss."

"Well, using the phrase 'post-coital' shatters mine."

"Then we're even. Can you sleep? For a little while?"

"I think. For a little while."

"I'm staying. Don't freak out."

"I'd love it if you stayed." *Truth?* She examined the statement even as she was spiraling down into a dreamless dark hole. *Yes. Truth.*

"**J**ust let her sleep, Jenny, will you for Christ's sake let her sleep?"

"But she might be sick!"

"She's not sick, she's tired, you get tired, right?"

"Dr. Rivers, will you please let me past before I get Mr. Krenklov and his Sig Sauer in here?"

"Keep your voice down!"

"For God's sake!" Alex said, opening her eyes and sitting up. "I can't believe you two woke me up! What *is* it?"

"It's ten o'clock in the morning, Princess," Jenny hollered over Shel's shoulder.

"Go back to sleep," Shel ordered.

Alex could see he was planted squarely in the doorway, and Jenny had to jump up to see into the room. She looked like an agitated, well-clad rabbit. "You've missed your first two appointments."

"It is *not* . . ." She blinked. Yes, that was sunlight. A lot of it. Sunlight. *Morning.* "Oh my God, I slept all night? And didn't . . ." She shut her mouth, though why she bothered she had no idea. Jenny certainly knew about the nightmares—there were no secrets in the Sitka palace, or at least not very many. And of course Shel knew. "Why—why didn't you wake me?"

Shel looked over his shoulder and quirked an eyebrow at her. "You're kidding, right?"

She flung the covers back and jumped out of bed. "Come in here and shut the door. Both of you. Oh my God. I've missed appointments!"

"Yeah, that sound you heard was the world *not* coming to an end," Shel snarked.

She ignored him, frantic, "Jenn, help me. Where's the yellow Donna Karan?"

"I have it right here. If Dr. Rivers will excuse us, we'll get you ready."

"I have to go," she said, rushing to him and giving him a distracted kiss as Jenny went to the closet for the shoes that matched the Karan. "I mean, I have to stay, but other people have to come up. I'm sorry. See you tonight?"

"Sure." He grinned. "At least put some underpants on before you start your first meet 'n' greet."

She looked down at herself. "Good advice."

Chapter 39

"... and tomorrow the king insisted you take the day off, so there really isn't anything on the schedule."

I can't believe I slept all night. In his arms, like some fairy tale princess. Which I certainly am not. No guns in fairy tales.

"And then, of course, we'll be test driving Ferraris and driving them off cliffs, à la Thelma and Louise."

And he was so great about it. He's been great about everything. He's so nice to me and he doesn't give a holy old crap about the money or the title or any of it. He didn't even want me to pay for his meal! He never wants me to pay for anything.

"Then we'll have sex change operations, and you will be Alan, and I'll be Jon."

"If I'm going to be a man, my name will be Fred, and very funny, Jenny. I heard everything you said."

"Perhaps you got too much sleep," she suggested slyly.

"Boy, that was weird, wasn't it?"

"..."

"What?"

"Nothing, Princess. If we're finished here, I can—"

"No, come on, let's hear it."

"Well." Jenny shifted her weight; she had clearly been

ready to get up from the small table, and now had to stay put. "I think part of your . . . difficulties . . . stem from being unable to give up control. But once you do that, you can relax."

Alex sniffed. "I don't think psychology is your field."

"No, but it certainly could be."

She bit her tongue so she wouldn't say something nastier. Of course, Jenny was wrong. It wasn't that cut-and-dried . . . what was? Oh, so she let Shel tie her up and fuck her and that's how she could come? Because it was all out of her control? And so was Shel? And once she gave up enough control she could sleep? How completely, totally, utterly ridiculous.

"Dr. Rivers has called," Jenny said, apropos of nothing. "He'll be here within the next thirty minutes."

"I—that's fine."

"And the king will see you for breakfast tomorrow."

"Where is he now?"

"Fishing with some locals."

"Of course. Should have guessed. Did he put on one of those dumb beards to disguise himself?"

"I didn't see him leave, Princess, but I would bet my clothing budget that you're right."

"He doesn't want me to do *anything* tomorrow?"

"Apparently not, Your Highness."

"That's weird, don't you think?"

"That you should have a day off? Highness, look who you're asking."

She laughed again. "Good point. Sorry. I don't suppose I could talk you into taking tomorrow off, too."

"Well . . . if you want me to . . ."

She blinked. What had Jenny just said? Was the universe about to implode as well? "You want tomorrow off?"

"No, no. Of course not. But then, if you don't think you'll *need* me . . ."

"Oh my God! You're into Teal Grange! *You're* into *Teal Grange*.*"* Talk about opposites attract! Not that she was in any position to judge. "That's great! Good for you. Of course, take tomorrow off, take my credit card, have a party."

"It's not Teal."

Whoa. She blinked. "Jenny, you're shockingly quick. We've been here, what? Less than two weeks? And you've got how many men on the string?"

"Not at all. His brother is in town. His identical twin, violin playing, doctorate at Berkeley brother." Jenny cupped her chin in her hands and sighed. "Ohhhhhh, his brother."

Alex stared for a moment, then recovered herself. "Well, that's great. That's—I mean, Teal's a great guy, but you guys didn't strike me as—I mean—have fun tomorrow."

"And you might as well know, Highness, I'll need some time off for the wedding."

So completely taken by surprise at the conversation, Alex didn't immediately follow. "You mean the invitation came? Elizabeth unbent?"

"No. My wedding."

"You've known this guy since . . ."

"Last night. We decided, after a 1947 Bordeaux, that we were going to be together forever." At the princess's flabbergasted expression, Jenny added, "Teal had a Zipfer."

"Jenny, whoa, put the brakes on! Are you sure you know what you're doing?"

"Yes."

"No, really."

"Yes, really, Your Highness."

"But you barely know the guy!"

"I know. Isn't it silly? But when you know, that's all there is." Jenny stacked some papers together and gave her boss a penetrating look. "There's no use fooling myself."

"Well . . . have a good day tomorrow . . . maybe you can bring him up. I'd love to meet him."

"Which reminds me, I must meet with the king. I have a first violin player ready to come help put together a Juneau orchestra. I would be grateful for any support you feel you can give us."

"Of—of course. I'll talk to Dad. He's always bitching because there's not enough culture in Juneau. Like he'd make it through a symphony without snoring."

"And your call to Her Majesty Queen Elizabeth will be going through in . . ." Jenny glanced at her watch. "Four minutes."

"Great. Thank you."

"I'll see Dr. Rivers up when he arrives."

"Great. Thank you."

"Princess, are you all right?"

"Oh, fine. There's just . . . a lot going on right now."

"Yes indeed," Jenny said cheerfully, and excused herself.

Chapter 40

"It's very good to hear from you, Alex. How is your dear niece?"

"Dara's great, Queen Elizabeth, thank you for asking. And thank you for speaking with me."

"It's my pleasure, dear. How may I help you?"

"Well . . . I wanted to congratulate you on William's upcoming wedding."

"A *lovely* girl." Pronounced, in the way of the upper British class, "gull." "An impeccable family. And she loves dogs; she has six of her own. Six!"

"Yes, she sounds wonderful. I—ah—I was wondering—I don't want to seem forward, but it seems like our invitation has been lost in the, uh, mail."

There was a pause. Alex plunged ahead. "And in case you were waiting for RSVPs, I didn't want you to think we weren't. RSVPing, I mean."

"Oh?" the queen managed.

"Because, unfortunately, I wanted to tell you that I'm afraid my family—not a *single member* of my family—can make it to Will's wedding. And I beg you not to be offended, and I apologize on behalf of the Baranovs."

"You—your father can't—you won't be able to come?"

"I'm afraid not, Your Majesty."

"Oh! That—that's unfortunate, dear. William will be so disappointed. I had been, ah, looking forward to introducing you all at the blessing."

"Maybe at Harry's wedding."

The queen laughed. "Bite your tongue, darling! I'm sorry about the invitation; I'll be sure to send another one round at once. These mails! Dreadful!"

"Really dreadful," Alex agreed, sprawling with relief in her chair. "Thank you again for taking my call."

"Say hello to King Alexander for me, darling. And you take care, too. May I say, and I hope you don't find me forward, but may I say I thought you looked after him splendidly after that nasty business last year." Naw-stee business lahst yeah. "A parent prays for a daughter like you, dear, and I hope your father appreciates what a gem you are."

"Oh," she managed. What an odd thing for the queen to say, and how happy it made her feel. "Thank you so much, Queen Elizabeth. I—I look after him as best I can."

"Yes, your duty to family has been impeccable—I've always thought so. And the new gull is charming. Just charming."

"Oh, Christina? Yes, she's . . ." The devil with blonde hair? No, that wouldn't do. ". . . great. Just great."

"Well, darling, if you're finished with me, I have to see about a few things."

It was hilarious, the way the queen pretended like she couldn't hang up anytime she wanted. Alex bit back a giggle that was half hysterical with relief. "Thank you again for your time. Please give my congratulations to William."

"I will, dear. Good day."

Just as she hung up her door opened and Sheldon stuck his head inside. "Tell me you weren't just gossiping with the Queen of England."

"Hardly. Grab Jenny, will you?"

He gave her a mock salute, vanished out of the doorway, then Jenny came into the room, Sheldon on her heels.

Jenny barely sketched the traditional bow before bursting out, "Well?"

"Cake. She'll send an invitation as long as none of us show up."

Jenny closed her eyes in brief relief. "Edmund and I will see that you're all far too busy."

"Wait a minute," Sheldon said. Alex saw he had no backpack. Why did that surprise, annoy, and thrill her, all at once? "That was the plan? To get an invitation but not do anything about it?"

"A brilliant plan," Jenny said, smiling at her boss.

"Your dad wanted to be invited but didn't want to go?"

"He hates those things. You've met him—he almost fell asleep during the last royal wedding, and that was his own son's."

"But he's not going to do anything with the invite? He's got that much pride?"

They just looked at him.

"Right, right. Dumb question."

Chapter 41

"**D**idn't you bring any toys?" she murmured, returning his wild kisses as they tumbled to the bed, rolling and tugging and stroking.

"No."

"Really?"

"Really."

"Nothing at all?"

"Not a single thing." He had her breasts bared and was kissing her nipples, and she wriggled out of her skirt and tugged on his pants. After much flailing of limbs, they were finally naked . . . or naked enough.

"Afraid of a strip-search?"

"No," he mumbled into her mouth. "Just another step in the plan."

"Um . . . what plan?"

"Tell you later," he said, gripping her wrists in his hands and pinning them over her head. His knee went between her thighs, forcing them wide for him, and he thrust into her. She gasped and surged to meet him, wrapping her legs around his waist and rocking against him. "Oh Christ . . . that's good . . . don't stop doing that . . ."

"I won't if you won't . . . oh, God . . ."

He captured her mouth again and again, kissing her so passionately, as if he hadn't seen her in a year rather than a day, and she returned his passion, his thrusts, and then trembled around him as her orgasm burst through her.

"Oh, *God*, that's nice," he said into her neck.

"You're . . . telling . . . me . . ." she panted. She wriggled a bit, but he had her wrists pinned firmly, and the thought— she couldn't get away, not if he didn't want her to, but nothing bad would happen, he'd never let anything bad happen—made her rock into another orgasm.

He stiffened above her and his breathing stopped for a moment. Then he collapsed against her shoulder with a groan.

After a moment, she whispered, "Are you going to let me go now?"

"Never," he replied.

Chapter 42

Nicky!

"Alex."

Get down!

"Alex." His hands, stroking her in the dark. "It's just a dream. Go back to sleep."

"Okay," she said fuzzily, and did.

"... I just think if you tried a nice Serena, or maybe a Majorero, you might be pleasantly surprised."

He had his hands clamped over his ears and was rolling back and forth on the bed, chanting, "La la la la la la la la!"

"I know you can hear me!" Alex shouted, leaning over him. "I'm not saying start with a blue, something really strong. Pick a mild one. It's no worse than Velveeta, and actually quite a bit better."

Shel cracked one eye open, but didn't remove his hands. "Are you done?"

"Yes, idiot."

"Because I've put up with a lot, Princess, but there are some things I will not do."

"*I* gave up insomnia for you."

"Totally different thing. And actually, I cured your insomnia. And your, uh, sex problem."

She was amused. "You cured me?"

"All part of my plan. If the handcuffs worked, we'd try that, then move to ties, then me, then nothing."

"Nothing? You mean masturbation?"

"No," he replied, not acknowledging her joke. "Like a real couple who love each other and don't need tricks to prove it."

She was speechless, and swallowed the lump that had suddenly appeared in her throat. "A—a couple in love? But we—I mean, I'm not going to be here forever . . ."

He said nothing; just looked at her.

"And—and I didn't think—I mean, I thought we were—"

"You let just any guy tie you up, then?" he asked coolly.

"No! You know I don't. You know you're the only man I ever—"

There was a discreet rap at the door. "Come in," Alex almost snarled, as Shel snatched a blanket to cover his nudity.

Jenny diffidently stepped into the bedroom. "I beg your pardon, Highness. Dr. Rivers. But Prince David is on the phone, and his schedule is very tight today. Will you take the call?"

"Yes. Put him through."

"Again, my apologies for disturbing you."

"We're kind of in the middle of something," Shel warned her. She ignored him, and picked up the phone when it rang.

"Hello?" She could see that Shel, disgusted, had gotten up and was hunting for his clothes. Oh, great. So much for their romantic day together.

"Alex? Hi! How's it going?"

"Everything's fine, David," she replied, ignoring Shel's glare. "How's Dara? How's Chris?"

"They're fine. Chris keeps showing her your TV appearances and that spread in *US* magazine about you. I think she recognizes you!"

"That's great. What's up?"

"Well, I just wanted to know why nobody's scheduled my trip. Edmund's not here, and my guy doesn't know a thing about it, and Jenny—"

"What are you talking about?"

"The Geneva thing got cancelled," her brother explained patiently. "Remember? I know Dad told you. So I can come out there and finish up. I mean, hell, the only reason you got stuck with it is because I was tied up with something else."

"Tied up?"

"Can you hear me okay? Is it a bad connection?"

"It's fine. Geneva was cancelled? He . . . Dad did mention something about it . . ." And she assumed he was kidding. He was not. In fact, it appeared he had dropped the entire issue. But why? To see what she would do? Or not do?

"Right. So, when do you want to come back?"

Don't do it.

"I can come back anytime."

"Yeah? I've got your schedule right here; looks like you've got a free day, you lucky jerk. You want to come back this afternoon? You could be eating at your own table for suppertime."

You'll be sorry.

"Absolutely."

"Okay, then. Have Jenn coordinate with the NDISL people and tell them I'll be out first thing in the morning."

You're ruining everything. Everything.

"I'll do that, gladly. It'll be good to be back home."

"I'll bet. Fish out of water there, huh? Not exactly your field. It was great of you to go and take one for the team."

"I was glad to, but it'll . . . it'll be good to be back. It's . . . it's been kind of a disaster.

You idiot.

Chapter 43

"**Y**ou *coward*."

Stung, and embarrassed, she cried, "You know I'm not! You know what I did!"

"Oh, sure," he sneered, "swing a chair and fracture the skull of a bad guy to save your family, great. Even a rabbit will fight if you pin them to the wall. But when it comes to actual hard emotional truth and bravery, you're on the first fucking plane out!"

"My job is done! I have to go back. The crown prince and the king said so."

"Oh, fuck the crown prince and the king! Like you couldn't stay if you really wanted to."

"Shel, I wasn't even supposed to be the one to come out here."

"Well, I'm sure as shit not going to fuck your brother when *he* shows up!" Shel roared.

"Good, because he's taken!"

"Don't you get it, you goddamned idiot? *So are you.*"

"Watch your mouth."

"So sorry, Princess Idiot."

"You know," she said through gritted teeth, "every once

in a while, it would be a *little* nice if you were just a tiny bit respectful of my title."

"Yeah, and a cure for cancer would be nice, too, but it's not in the cards for a while."

"Shel, it's not just me."

"Ha!"

"You've never even said—not in so many words . . . You've been having a good time, too, just like me. Right?" she added tentatively.

"Yeah? You want the words? No problem. I love you. I love you like no one in my life, and I'll never love anyone like I love you again, ever. *I love you.* There." He crossed his arms over his chest and added with pure contempt, "Now let's watch you break a speed record getting to the door."

She ground her teeth. Had she ever been so thrilled, terrified, furious, and happy at the same time? She was so dizzy she was afraid she'd vomit. And she'd rather split a tooth than cry in front of him. "You don't even know me."

"Right."

"And I don't know you."

Except that he was the finest, most maddening man in the world. That he whispered her name in the dark and ate all the peas on her plate. That he resented his father and revered his mother. That he hated being the new kid when he was in school. That he thought she was beautiful and smart and sexy. That he wanted to be with her. That he hated not spending the night.

With her. Only with her.

She took a breath. "Are you really telling me you're going to move? Again? You want the happily ever after? You want to uproot, change everything, move to Alaska of all places, where you'll be rich—*Prince* Sheldon—and your son will be a prince, and all your grandchildren?"

He opened his mouth, and she could instantly see he had never thought of it in those terms. He'd been so focused on having her, he'd never considered the fact that he'd have to give up everything to do it.

"I didn't think so," she said triumphantly, and then started to cry. "Don't you dare!" she shouted when he took a hesitant step forward. "You get your pants on and get out of here!"

"Is that a royal command?" he asked hoarsely, pale as the sheets.

"Take it however you want. Just get out."

"Fine, Princess. Nice fucking you."

"Lovemaking!" she yelled as he hopped out the door, struggling to get his right leg into his left pant leg. "It was lovemaking, and don't you ever forget it!"

Chapter 44

She'd broken the last lamp when the gentle tapping became insistent pounding. "Get lost!" she yelled, kicking one of the delicate side tables into the wall. "No visitors, Jenny, I don't care if it's the new Pope!"

"How about the king of Alaska?" a familiar voice said through the door.

"Not now, Dad!" She booted another table.

"Aw, come on, honey, you're costing me a fortune in there."

"Take it out of one of my trust funds!"

"Open this door."

She tried to make her mouth say "go away," but her training and background were too strong. She could no more ignore an order from her father—or the king—than she could attend a press conference without a shirt.

She trudged to the door and opened it, then waded through the detritus her rage had made and flopped face-down on the bed.

"Jee-zus," her father whistled, tripping over a broken lamp. "It looks like Guns N' Roses were in here with you."

"You're dating yourself, Dad. They broke up. It's the way of the world: desertion and despair."

"What?"

She rolled over so she was no longer mumbling into her pillow. "What can I do for you, my king?"

"Uh . . . live happily ever after?"

"I was thinking more a short-term project."

"How about getting something on besides that robe? It's almost noon. You can have lunch with your old man."

"I've got a plane to catch."

"Yeah, uh, about that . . . I guess the boy isn't coming with you?"

"Not hardly."

"Too bad."

"Dad. You hated him."

"No, I admired the shit out of him. But I covered it up real good," he bragged. He picked up an intact chair and set it beside the bed, then plopped into it. "How many times are you gonna meet someone who likes you—"

"For who I am, not what I have, blah-blah."

"No, I meant, likes you *despite* who you are."

"Oh, that's a nice thing to say," she snapped.

"You want nice? Get Jenny in here, she'll fill you up with it. I'm a truth guy."

"Says the man who sneaks on fishing boats in disguise."

"That's because I have a hard time finding people who like me for who I am," he said bluntly, "and do you get where I'm going with this, or do I haveta get Edmund in here with the crayons?"

"God, not Edmund, too. I couldn't face both of you."

"In that case, good luck," her father said quietly, "looking in the mirror."

"What, Dad, what?" She propped herself up on her elbows. "You're saying I should tell him I love him and whisk him away to Alaska?"

"Well—"

"First of all, he won't go. Second, if he did go, he'd never let his kids be, as he puts it, 'rich assholes.' And I'll never give up my family duties. Never."

"No," he said quietly. "I wouldn't expect you to. And maybe the boy doesn't, either."

"It was stupid, stupid, stupid. I never meant for this to happen. I should never have—" She closed her mouth.

"Alex, sometimes this stuff . . . it's beyond your control. But that doesn't make it a bad thing."

"Dad, beyond my control is the very definition of bad."

"Come on. Anybody who can brain a traitor and knock him out with one swing can adjust to change. I mean, Jesus. It's not like self-defense and attempted regicide was on the schedule that day," the king joked.

She stared at him. "It's not funny, Dad."

"Well. It's a little funny."

"No."

"Jeez, kid, is that what this is about? Because you like everything on the schedule, all the time? How'd you get to twenty-three—"

"Twenty-five."

"—without realizing some stuff will never, ever be planned?"

She opened her mouth, and nothing came out.

"See, that's why I'm the smart one," he said smugly.

"You are not. It goes me, David, Kathryn, Nicky, Alexander, and you."

"Like hell! Punks."

"And things can be planned," she insisted. "It doesn't have to be chaotic."

"It's my fault," the king decided. "It's no way to bring up a kid."

"Don't be an idiot."

"Wave and smile and sign this and break the champagne

bottle on that, and at eight-oh-two we'll have cheese omelets with the American President, and at nine-oh-seven we'll visit the new elementary school named after your mother . . ."

"Dad, come on. It's how it is. Your childhood was like that, and so was Grandpa's. You know the upside—we never have to worry about paying the electric bill, never in our lives."

"Alex, you get that you didn't do anything wrong that day, right?"

"Yes."

"I mean, *really* get it? Because you were a good girl and a patriot, too, and that coward got what he deserved, and if you hadn't done it, your brother would have."

"Which one?"

"Either. Listen, Dr. Pohl told me—"

"Nothing, I assume, due to doctor-patient privilege."

"It was a hypothetical."

"Oh, hypothetical. My ass."

"Anyway, she says, even though you didn't have to face any consequences—like being arrested or what-have-you— she says that doesn't mean there weren't any consequences at all."

"I might have heard something like that," she admitted. "But how did we get on this topic? You were lecturing me on my love life a minute ago."

"Sweetie, if you haven't figured out how it's all related, than you're not the smart one. At all."

"We were talking about how I was stupid to let Shel get away," she said in a monotone.

"I didn't use the word stupid. And you've got to stop punishing yourself for what happened last year. Look what it's costing you! Insomnia was bad enough, the dreams were bad enough, not being able to let an hour go by without checking on the baby was bad enough."

"Dad—"

"Now you're running away, and for what? So you can go back to bad dreams and worrying about the next assassination attempt? Bullshitting Dr. Pohl because you know what the problem is, you just can't face it?"

"I can't handle this right now, Dad." She put a hand over her eyes. She hadn't cried in front of him since the hospital. Twice in one day? Both in front of men she wanted to impress? No no no. "I really can't."

"Looks like you don't have to. Because you're on a plane, and the boy's staying put. Everything can go on the way it's supposed to. Safe and sane and scheduled."

"He won't come anyway, Dad. And I'm not exactly in a job I can quit."

"No," he allowed, "but did you ask him?"

"He won't."

"Well, nothing to be done about it, then."

She peeked at him from between her fingers. He looked deceptively innocent. "That's right," she said. "Nothing to be done."

He pulled a piece of dental floss from his pocket and she rolled over, away from the horror. The final, complete horror, the official point of no return: the worst day of the year. Second worst of her life.

Chapter 45

"**O**h. My. God." Teal was gaping around Sheldon's lab. "Who'd you kill?"

"Get lost," he suggested warmly.

"Oh, Sheldon," Crane said, gingerly crunching across broken glass. "The soul of politeness, even in the depths of being dumped."

"Hey, hey! I dumped her. Hi, by the way."

"Big bro had this nutty idea that it'd be nice to see you again," Teal said, jerking a thumb at his twin, who had an expression on his face as if he was smelling a room full of elephant droppings. "I told him you'd be an asshole about it, seeing as how Alex's plane left a while ago, but he's a moron. So here we are."

"It's nice to see you again," Shel sighed. He was lying prone in the corner, on a bed of equipment requisition paperwork. "How's things going?"

"Er, fine. I'm sorry I didn't get to meet the princess."

"It's overrated. How long you in town?"

"Not long." Crane took off his glasses, pulled a small, gray cloth out of his breast pocket, polished them, then settled them back on his nose. "I'm moving to Alaska next week."

Shel sat up. A req form for a centrifuge stuck to his back. "You're *what?*"

"In addition to having your heart broken, did someone rupture your eardrums? I said I'm moving."

Sheldon blinked. He was used to Crane being a little on the weird side, but this? "To Alaska?"

"Of course. My fiancée lives there, and she's even now using her contacts to secure a job for me. First chair," he added smugly.

"And you're just—you're just going? Who's your fiancée?" he asked dumbly.

"Jenny," the Grange twins said in unison.

"Jenny? *Jenny* Jenny? Alex's Jenny? Who you only met, like, sixteen hours ago? *That* Jenny?"

"It's been longer than that," Crane said.

"And they haven't even done it!" Teal said gleefully.

"Wh—but—why—" Shel brushed the paper off and tottered to his feet. "But you live in Boston! You've got the nicest apartment I've ever seen! You put down roots! You've got pussy thrown at you from cars!"

"Stop shouting, I'm right here. And ugh, by the way."

"You're just picking up and going? Turning your back on your whole life? To live with someone you barely know?"

"Why are you saying things out loud? Everyone in the room already has this information."

"Has everybody gone *crazy?*" Shel yelled at the ceiling.

"Hey, I tried to talk him out of it," Teal said, kicking over an overturned file cabinet just to hear the noise. "Okay, I didn't. What do I give a shit if he lives in Boston or Juneau? He'd be annoying if he lived in Moscow. And by the way, I am *not* helping you clean this shit up."

"Just like that?" Shel mused.

"There's no point in waiting," Crane said, "or letting

some other gentleman realize what a fine woman she is. I'm not getting any younger, certainly."

"You're twenty-nine."

"You can tell," Teal said, "by all the grotesque wrinkles on the jackass's face." He turned to his brother. "By the way, you owe me huge. Not only did I introduce you to your wife, I didn't bone her."

"The thank-you note is already in the mail."

"I can't believe this!" Sheldon said, raking his fingers through his hair.

"I'd invite you to the wedding," Crane went on with his trademark maddening calm, "but you'll likely be too busy sulking in this opium den to attend."

"Oh, that's just great! She got in a plane and took off. I told her I loved her and she was all 'oh, that's just the hormones talking, gotta go, my jet's waiting.' What the hell was I supposed to do?"

"Stop being a dick," Teal said at the same moment that Crane said, "Go after her."

"What? She didn't even tell me she loves me. And she *left*."

"Not unlike another beloved family member."

"Oh, cram it up your ass, Crane! This isn't about my father. It's about us and how we'd never work."

"Because you've, like, tried super hard to make it work, instead of just showing up at her hotel room to bone her," Teal said.

"You can cram it up your ass, too. You don't know anything about what we—just shut up, both of you."

"So that's it? You're just gonna let the most eligible babe on the planet, who lets you do pretty much whatever you want to her, who thinks you're the swellest guy around, at least according to the *National Enquirer*—"

"Swellest?" Crane asked.

"—you're just gonna let her go back to her palace and—what? You're gonna find someone else? Who's gonna be better than her? Because, pal, if she was out there, you prob'ly would have found her by now."

"Get it through your head," Shel snapped, "both of you. She left me. She wouldn't even stay the day, and it was her day off!"

"Yeah, she's so stubborn, you guys have nothing in common."

"A disguised miracle," Crane agreed, "that she left town."

Shel blew out a breath. The twins were aggravating beyond belief, as usual, but their logic was starting to penetrate. He'd already endured three hours knowing Alex was gone forever; he didn't relish picturing what the rest of his life was going to be like.

But . . .

"Look, why should I go after her? Why can't she come back and just admit that we have something? Why do I have to be the one to make it easy for her? I mean, she's got everything. Money, and power, and her dad's a king, for God's sake."

"And in return, all she has to put up with is someone occasionally trying to kill a family member, and giving up most of her privacy—she can't go to the movies, grocery shopping, or the park."

"Seems like a decent trade to me," Teal agreed. "You don't have to worry about the rent, just the occasional assassination attempt."

"Really, she has it very easy."

"Totally," Teal agreed.

"So—what? You're saying I should go after her and, you know, tell her we can work it out? Give up my job, my home? Move again? Be the goddamned Prince of Alaska?"

"Assuming she'll have you."

"Big assumption," Teal added.

"You're saying I should take a chance? That maybe it'll work out?"

"No," Crane said. "*You're* saying." He glanced at his watch. "Either way, I must be going. Jenny and I have a date tonight."

"Because I can't just hop a plane to Alaska and barge into the palace. For one thing, I'll probably get shot, or stabbed. The place is lousy with guards. For another, if they don't get me, Alex will. We, uh, didn't exactly part on good terms."

"I'll bet you implied *she* was the coward."

"Because, of course, you're a dick," Teal said cheerfully.

"Goddammit!"

"I think he's having an epiphany," Crane told his brother.

"I had that once. But the doctor gave me a shot and it went away."

"You—enjoy your date. You—drive me to my apartment. I've got to have my goddamned passport to get on the god-damned plane to goddamned Alaska."

"Aw," Teal said. "That's so fuckin' romantic."

Chapter 46

"I really really really appreciate this," Shel told Jenny for the hundredth time.

"It's my great pleasure, Dr. Rivers. And I hope, after the princess terminates me, you'll help me find work."

"She'd never do that," Shel said. "You're like family."

"Really?" Jenny seemed pleased.

"She told me."

"It's always nice to hear the truth out loud."

"Not always," Shel murmured, turning to look out the window. North Dakota was falling away from them and he closed his eyes and tried not to picture flaming fuselage.

"I can't wait to see your home, my dear. I've never been to Alaska."

"Crane, you'll love it. It's the most beautiful place in the entire world."

"As beautiful as your eyes, my little ballerina?"

"Kill me now," Shel muttered, glaring into the postcard-beautiful sky.

Jenny had arranged everything. Crane, that sly dog, had

called her while Shel was frantically searching for his passport. By the time they'd gotten to the airport, she'd arranged seats for them and fixed everything with customs, the pilot, and Alaskan Air Control.

"What a stroke of luck you were still in the country," Crane was babbling.

"Well . . . Her Highness left too quickly, I had a few things to arrange before I could follow her. And I didn't want to miss our date," she said shyly.

"Never! I'd sooner miss the opening of Rachmininoff's Piano Concerto number two."

Jenny giggled. "Do you know, when I was younger—"

"A doddering nineteen?"

"—I would be so uplifted by his music that I mistook the feeling for—for—you know."

"I shall have to play it for you when we're alone," he murmured.

"No, really," Shel whispered to the window. "Kill me right now."

"You should be working on your apology," Crane informed him, cutting himself off in mid-smooch.

"Me?" he yelped.

"Oh, knowing you, you said some perfectly atrocious things and now you're expecting her to apologize for your bad behavior."

"Right," Jenny added. "You should be ashamed, Dr. Rivers."

"I'm throwing you both off the plane if you don't get off my case right now."

"That doesn't sound very contrite."

"No, it doesn't," Jenny sniffed.

"Now, if it were you, turtledove, I would be on bended knee," Crane cooed, staring into Jenny's eyes with the rapt expression of a George Romero zombie. "I would ask the gods for your so-kind forgiveness."

"Oh, Crane, really?" she breathed. "I would give it. In a heartbeat, I would give it!"

"Oh, God," Shel said, looking back out the window.

Chapter 47

"Welcome back, Jenny," Marin said warmly. "The palace isn't the same without you."

"What a lie, Marin. And thank you. Please log me in as of twenty-three-hundred hours. I'm also bringing these gentlemen up with me. This is Mr. Grange, and this is Dr. Rivers."

"I don't think I can do this," Shel said, looking around the grandeur of the castle's west foyer. It was bigger than his apartment, times five. "This is not my thing."

"Don't take the coward's way out now," Crane said. Bastard. He'd played in concert halls around the world, and for the Queen of England. He was used to this fancy shit. "You've come all this way."

"Dr. Rivers . . . Dr. Rivers . . ." Marin, the receptionist/guard/whatever was squinting at him. "You look familiar, Doctor. Have you been to the palace before?"

"*Minot Daily News,*" Crane said. "Page one."

"Oh. Oh! Dr. Rivers!" Marin started to fumble for the phone. "Of course, I didn't recognize you without a threatening upraised fist. You're not on the list, but I'm sure it will be all right. Let me just notify Her Highness—"

"Please don't do that," Jenny interrupted. "It's a surprise."

"Jenny, you know I can't do that."

"Trust me," Shel said, "if you call her, it's all over."

"What's all over?"

"Jenny!"

They all turned at the boyish shout. Sheldon immediately recognized the youngest Baranov, Prince Nicholas.

"Your Highness," Jenny said, bowing. Marin stood and also bowed. "It's past your bedtime, Prince Nicky."

"Jenny, I'm fourteen years old. I'll tell myself when to go to bed, okay?" He tried to sound tough, but with the angelic blond curls and large blue eyes, couldn't pull it off. Impulsively, he hugged her. "Welcome back."

"Your Highness, this is—"

"Dr. Rivers!"

"Uh, yes. Dr. Rivers, this is Prince Nicholas Baranov, sixth in line to—"

"Oh my God, you're *here!*" The young prince—just entering that lanky stage of all height, no weight—goggled at him. "Alex is going to *shit.*"

"Language, Your Highness."

"Sorry, Jenn, but she is."

"Actually," Jenny said, eyeing Marin, who was still standing beside her desk, "there seems to be some question as to whether he can come up . . ."

"He can come up," the prince said, doing a startling imitation of his father's cool, used-to-being-obeyed tone. *They must teach them that when they're baby royals,* Shel mused. "He absolutely can. Alex has been crying her—I mean, she's been really upset. I know she wants to see him. I don't know about you, though," he added, sizing Crane up.

"I beg your pardon, Prince Nicky. This is my fiancé, Crane Grange."

Nicky frowned. "I guess I missed some memos."

Crane shook his hand. "It's nice to meet you, Prince Nicholas. Jenny's told me a lot of wonderful things about you."

"It wasn't a bomb, by the way," the prince said. "Don't believe everything you read."

"If you'll sign here, sir," Marin said, extending a clipboard in Sheldon's direction.

He took it, and signed in as a guest. "Just like that, huh?" he asked, handing it back.

Nicky grinned. "Just like that."

Chapter 48

"Come," she called, grateful for the interruption. She needed a break from the pacing. Not to mention the crying. The palace was the same, but nothing else was.

Oh, and now she was hallucinating. Because it looked like Sheldon was walking through her door. Her suite. In the palace. Where he would never ever go. Because he—

"I'm ready," he said, stopping three feet in front of her, "to listen to your apology."

She stared.

"Also," he added, "I'm ignoring the fact that your little 'apartment' is bigger than the NDISL."

She stared some more.

"Well?" he demanded, hands on his hips. "Aren't you going to say a thing? Did I mention how much I hate flying? Because I fucking hate it. And not only was I facing death by horrifying crash every second I was on the plane, I had to watch Jenny and Crane make goo-goo eyes at each other. For hours! So you'd better say something."

"Is that an apology?" she managed.

"Forget it," he snapped. "You left. I said I love you, and you were leavin' on a jet plane like a bad Peter, Paul, and Mary song."

"Well, I love you, too," she snapped, "but I knew better than to say so!"

"Oh yeah?" He was shrugging out of his coat. "You could have fooled me."

"Oh, like you were going to quit your job and move and be a prince. Next thing you know, you'll be ordering brie as a dessert course." She yanked off her robe.

"That's a totally different issue," he insisted, unbuckling his belt. "I put myself out there and you left. Didn't even say it back."

"Well, I wanted to!" She pulled her nightgown over her head. "How could I ask you to move again, knowing you hate it so much? Knowing you were so happy at the NDISL? I love you, so I let you go."

"That's nice for a cross-stitch sampler," he said, kicking out of his shoes and slacks and unbuttoning his shirt, "but this is real life. And in real life, when someone you love says 'I love you,' you say it back."

"Well, I love you."

"Okay."

"Okay." She looked down at his feet. "You're going to take off your socks, right?"

"Hell, no, it's freezing in this place."

She laughed and rushed into his arms. "It's almost summer."

"Oh, God. Let's not talk about it."

They tumbled into her bed, her solitary bed, lonely no more, and kissed like reunited lovers—which they were—and purred and stroked each other, and whispered words of sweetness, of love, and the only thing that held her down was nothing, and it was all very fine.

And she came, and cried, and apologized, and he came, and kissed her tears away, and apologized, and held her, and she held him, and she was in love, and it was beyond all, it was like coming home. Finally, oh finally, she was home.

Chapter 49

"Can't I be your consort?" Shel begged. "Do I have to be a prince?"

"It's not so bad," David said. He had returned from North Dakota that morning, and the whole family was together for lunch. Dara and Sheldon had taken an instant dislike to each other, and they were both giving each other guarded looks from across the table. "There's an excellent dental plan, for example."

"Sorry," Al said. "Believe me, you don't look like a prince. At all. I'd make you the Duke of Shit if I could."

"Now that's got a nice ring to it," Alex's sister Kathryn said. Sheldon could see the promise of immense gorgeousness in the brunette teenager, and briefly pitied his future father-in-law. "The Duke of Shit! Think what the family crest would look like."

Nicky laughed and spit pea soup out of his nose. Dara laughed, too, and drooled peas down her chin, to be swiftly wiped up by her mother.

"Sorry, Shel," Alex said with real sympathy. "By law, the spouse of the prince or princess is himself (or herself) a prince or princess. And I might as well tell you, you're going to get stuck with a bunch more titles, too."

"Like Lord of Losers," Kathryn suggested.

"And by the way, if we're celebrating my official engagement," Alex demanded, "why are we serving a vegetable I hate?"

"Quitcher bitching," the king ordered. "They're cheap this time of year. You know what it costs to feed all you bums?"

"I have the figure, sir," Edmund said, standing very properly at the king's right elbow.

"That's okay," Shel said hastily. "I don't want to know."

"I also have the figures on what it cost to ship your things from North Dakota."

Alex frowned at him. "I told you I'd pay for that."

"And I told you to forget about it. Bad enough I've got maids and—and footmen and someone's secretly folding my socks. I mean, I'm freaking out just sitting in this room. Although, it helps that you're all kind of jerky. If you were stiff and proper, this would be a lot worse."

"I think the Duke of Shit just insulted us," Christina said.

"Language, please, Your Highness."

"Cram it, Edmund."

"Speaking of stiff and proper," Jenny said hastily from Alex's right elbow, "if I may, the invitation to Prince William's wedding came in the morning packet."

"I told you!" the king said, stopping in mid gnaw on his lamb chop to crow. "I knew she couldn't say no to me. Us, I mean."

"Unfortunately, sir, you're already scheduled to be in New York that day to address the U.N. It is not a thing to be rearranged."

"Right, right. Well, I'll call her."

"No need," Edmund said hastily. "I have already extended regrets on the family's behalf."

"Okay, then. We got any more a' these chops?"

"Dad, for God's sake," Kathryn said, rolling her eyes. "We're all still on the soup course."

"It's my fault you're all slow, like cows in a pasture?"

"That's great," Alex muttered.

"He called us all cows," Prince Alexander said and, to Shel's startlement, continued in verse:
"Another way of saying
I love you, children."

"You stop that," Kathryn ordered. "You haven't done the haiku thing in ages. You're just showing off for Sheldon."

"You guys are *so* weird," Shel said, staring into his soup. "I can't believe I gave up nice, sane North Dakota for this."

"Ah, but you did," Alex said, squeezing his leg under the table. "Remind me to thank you again later."

"Gross!" Kathryn, Alexander, and Nicky all screamed in unison.

"Not until you're married," the king said, "or I break your spine, boy. Possibly in more than one place."

"You're killin' me," Shel groaned, in a credible imitation of the king.

"It's awful, I know. But look at this, this is nice," Christina said, admiring the announcement in the *Juneau News*. "You actually don't look like you're going to hit the photographer."

"He caught me in a weak moment," Shel admitted. A post-coital moment, in fact. But what the king didn't know wouldn't hurt him. "If we can't do it until we're married," he informed his bride-to-be, "then the date just moved up by six months."

She grinned. He expected a protest, but all she said was, "I'll have Jenny send out an updated press release."

"No way!" the king hollered. "You know what I'll lose in deposits if you change the date?"

"You can't let them," Nicky said, "just so they can *do it*. Yech!"

"Shut up and finish your soup," Alex snapped.

"Your love life is yech.
We must never speak of this
Never in our lives."

"Alexander, I'm serious. If you don't stop with that, and I mean *right now* . . ." Kathryn brandished her empty soup bowl threateningly.

"That's amazing," Shel said. "They just come out of you? That's haiku?"

"You bet your ass it is," Prince Alexander said. "Give me any topic and I'll give you a great fuckin' haiku."

The king pointed his fruit fork at the prince. "You just watch your mouth, boy. You're not too big to spank. Or imprison."

"It's really a nice announcement," Christina said. She glanced at the princess. "You warned him, right? I mean, his pic's gonna be in all the magazines."

"I warned him."

"And the wedding coverage! You warned him he'd be on TV, right?"

"It's all right," Shel said. "Well, it's not, but it's worth putting up with."

Alex beamed. "I can't wait." She looked at her prince. "I love you."

"I love you, too," he said, touched. It was the first time she'd said it outside of the privacy of her rooms.

It made ignoring the faux-barfing noises from the younger royals very easy.

Chapter 50

"The Royal Household of Baranov, including His Majesty King Alexander II, announces the joyous occasion of the engagement of Her Highness, Princess Alexandria Baranov, to Dr. Sheldon Rivers, an American citizen.

"The wedding will take place at the Sitka Palace on Saturday, October 23rd, 2006, at 9:00 A.M. An expected eight thousand wedding invitations will be extended.

"The wedding will be held on the Sitka palace grounds and the reception will be on the West Lawn, weather permitting.

"All at the Sitka Palace wish life-long happiness to Her Highness the Princess of Alaska, and Dr. Rivers, future Prince of Alaska.

"After her wedding, Her Highness has announced her legal name and title will be Her Highness, Alexandria Baranov Rivers."

Chapter 51

One week later . . .

Scott Gottlieb fussed around Dr. Pohl's desk for a minute, waiting for his boss to come in. She tended to sleep late, then work until ten o'clock at night. That suited his schedule fine, as this job, cool as it was, was just a stopping point until he saved up enough to buy his own flower shop. He had the spot picked out: there was a lot just half a mile from the Sitka Palace, and one thing the Baranovs were famous for was convenience. If he could just get his shop set up there . . . he'd have enough funding in another year, maybe two. And his old man had promised to help him with the down payment on the lot this summer . . .

As Dr. Pohl's assistant, he got to see the business side of things and, even better, had hopes of spotting a royal. Although, Dr. Pohl usually went to the Sitka if she was supposed to see one of them . . . other than that time with Princess Christina, the Baranovs didn't come here, and why should they? Still, he had hopes . . .

His boss came in, hung up her duck-patterned jacket (mergansers), and held out the tray of hot drinks she'd grabbed from the local Starbucks. (She'd threatened to strangle him with the cord to the shades if he ever brought her coffee, and he believed her.) She sat down behind her desk as he took his (white hot chocolate with a shot of espresso) and placed hers (coffee, no cream, two sugars) on the desk blotter.

"Hi, Scott."

"Morning, Dr. Pohl. The mail's here. And so's your ten o'clock."

"That's 'Mrs. Johanssen,' Scott, they have names," she corrected him gently.

He colored. "Sorry, doc."

"Try not to do it again, please. I did see her on my way in, so just pop the mail in my bin and I'll get to it—"

"Uh, excuse me, Doctor, but there's something in there I think you should—I mean, it's from the palace."

"Our palace?" she asked, arching white eyebrows. She glanced over and there it was: a heavy, cream-colored envelope with the royal seal (a roaring lion holding a red shield) embossed on the back.

Dr. Pohl picked it up, turned it over to see who it was from (HRH AB was the only hint she got), slit it open with her duck letter opener (a mallard), eased out the sheet of stationery, paper so heavy it had to have some cloth in it, and started to read.

Scott pretended to straighten her files in the corner, then spun around when the doctor burst into tears.

"What's the matter?" he gasped. "Are you in trouble?" He had visions of King Al's troops bursting in to drag the doctor away for . . . what? He had no idea.

"No," Dr. Pohl sobbed. "I'm going to be a bridesmaid."

"Please, please can I come with?" he begged.

"No," Dr. Pohl said, still crying.

Chapter 52

Six months later . . .

"**I** can't believe this," Shel said. "I can't fucking believe it."

"Yep," his future sister-in-law said cheerfully. "The big day is finally here. I couldn't hardly sleep at all last night! Two royal weddings in two years! Too cool."

He grunted and looked down at her, then looked away. Since the braces had come off and her acne had cleared up, Kathryn's promise of beauty had been fulfilled, and now she looked disturbingly like a shorter version of Alex. She was wearing what all the bridesmaids wore, a ridiculously full-skirted crimson gown with what had to be three hoop skirts—the skirt came out to *here*. It was like something out of *Gone with the Wind*, a novel he loved mostly because all the rich people ended up poor.

The crimson bodice was studded with small red beads, and Kathryn was wearing a matching bead choker around her neck and ruby dangling earrings.

Her black hair was pinned up, showing the creamy perfection of her shoulders. If she was wearing shoes, Shel couldn't see them. Alex, his love, his bride, his (groan) princess, called them "meringue dresses" after a movie she had seen.

Kathryn's bouquet, a striking cluster of deep red calla lilies held together with a wide crimson ribbon, was carelessly discarded in the corner while she fussed over Sheldon's already immaculate tie.

"You look really terrific," he told her. "Really, uh, really beautiful."

"Well, finally," she said. "I've been waiting. You watch, I'll be the one having all the adventures next. I'm tired of David and Chris and Alex hogging the spotlight."

"Your dad might have something to say about that... you're only, what? Sixteen?"

"Oh." She dismissed the king of Alaska with a wave of her hand. "He has something to say about everything."

"I just can't believe any of this," he said, looking around his small dressing room. He'd spent most of his days in Minot, tying up loose ends and bringing the new head of the NDISL up to speed while he ducked the servants and guards. He'd shooed away his man servants—paid friends? Butlers? Whatever the hell they were called. He was supposed to have, like, ten, and he didn't need any.

"Can't believe what?" Kathryn asked.

"Huh? Oh, right. I can't believe we agreed to have an outdoor reception in October. In Alaska."

"Note the dresses," she said, pointing to her gigantic full skirt. "This thing might as well be made of Goretex; I can't feel a thing. And all the guys have on long pants and long sleeves, and your tuxes are wool."

"I noticed," he said, tugging at his sleeve. But it was good wool; he didn't really itch. It was nerves. Awful, horrible, unending nerves. The tuxes were actually pretty nice... dark gray, with a stripe on each leg, but done well enough so that he didn't feel like a waiter.

And Alex had insisted—no flower boutonnieres. Said they were tacky and everyone did them, which nearly caused a fistfight with Christina. Instead, the men were wearing inch-wide wreaths made of thyme. Although he had not been consulted (he'd made clear he had no desire to plan any of it, except for one detail which Alex had readily agreed to, thank God) he liked them. Alex was right: in a wedding where tradition ruled, it was nice to see new things.

"And the sun is out!" Kathryn was still babbling. "It's going to be a gorgeous fall day. Nobody's gonna be cold."

Then why was cold sweat trickling down his shoulder blades? Obviously, nothing to do with the weather . . .

"And don't forget," his future sister-in-law reminded him, "you also promised my dad you wouldn't have sex until after you were married."

"Mind your own business," he said automatically, "you little creep." Since his dick got hard, to paraphrase Eddie Murphy, when the wind blew, Shel needed no such reminding. The king had caught them at a weak moment, making them swear on their honor: no gropey until after the wedding-ey. And Alex, damn her Baranov sense of duty, had made them stick to it. Agh! It was the longest he'd gone without sex in . . . er . . .

"So!" Kathryn added, still straightening his tie, which was already perfectly straight, "you must be really really glad today is here finally, huh?"

"Actually, the time really, uh, flew." And it had. It had rushed up at him, like a wild animal free of its leash. It seemed like it had just been spring a week ago. Now he was about to be the Prince of Alaska. Because the only way to get the only woman in the world he wanted was to get a crown.

A goddamned crown!

"Are you all right?" Kathryn asked. "You look kind of pukey."

"I feel kind of pukey," he admitted. "I'm going to walk around outside for a couple of minutes."

She held his wrist and looked at his watch, a gift from the

king. "You've got about twenty before you're supposed to be in South Juneau."

He shivered. They named the big ballrooms, halls, parlors, whatever, after towns in the country. South Juneau sounded like a conference room, but it was really a gigantic dance hall that could hold thousands. "Don't remind me," he said, and slouched off.

Everyone left him alone—the palace grounds were safe enough, and he was on the opposite side . . . all the guests were streaming into the place from the north.

He stood and watched the bees (a phrase he'd picked up from Nicky and, dammit, they were people, he had to stop calling them "castlebees" in his head) setting up for the reception. It looked like there were bowls and bowls of flowers just . . . everyplace. And since the ceremony was going to be brief (thank you, thank you God), they were already setting food out, protectively covered.

He grinned to see the stacks and stacks of miniature hot dogs—in wee buns an inch long!—and hamburgers, and mini lobster rolls. He could see the cakes being rolled out to their tables: a four-tiered groom's cake (they had made an extra one for the wedding as well as the rehearsal banquet) in dark chocolate, and decorated with thin white ribbons circling each tier.

And *the* cake, the one Christina had insisted on making and decorating: four enormous Swiss vanilla tiers covered in ice-blue frosting—but it was that flat kind of frosting— fondue? Fondant? Anyway, it looked as smooth as an ice pond, and had been decorated with sugared pine cones and chocolate twigs. He wasn't a sweets person, but the cake really was something. He could have gobbled half a tier on his own, if he wasn't scared he'd puke.

He got a little closer, puzzled because he kept seeing the

same set of initials on everything: BR. Hanging banner-like from trees, on tables, on doors and windows—Rough? Bring Roses?

It hit him: duh. Baranov/Rivers. That was . . . nice. He guessed. Okay, it was a little creepy. He was sure someone had told him his and Alex's initials would be splashed all over everything on the big day, but to see it in real life was . . . weird.

"Hey! Loser!"

"Sheldon! Over here!"

He looked; there were the Grange twins in all their tuxedo'd glory—he couldn't remember Teal ever wearing anything but a T-shirt and jeans. He grinned; truly a momentous occasion.

"Thanks for the real food," Teal said with his mouth full as Shel approached. "Have you had one of these baby hot dogs? They're awesome!"

In response to a pleading look from one of the caterers, Shel said, "Knock it off, assface. Those're for the reception."

"Hey, we're guests of honor," Teal bragged, while his twin helped the caterer cover the hot dogs.

"True, but keep your ham-handed fingers off the food until it's time."

"I must admit, you're the best looking valet I've ever seen," Crane teased.

"Shut your cake hole. Both of you." He pressed the heels of his hands to his eyes. "Why didn't I elope?"

"Because Alex never would have agreed. She's all about duty, that girl."

"Don't remind me." The three friends fell silent and watched the caterers filling long clear vases with white calla lilies and place them on the tables. Kathryn had been right; the weather was a miracle. Lots of sun, no wind. It could have been August instead of early fall.

He stared down at the closest table, reading the top of the little box which served as a treat and a place holder, the name written in beautiful, spidery black script: Susan Sarandon. Oh, for Christ's sakes. That couldn't be right, could it? How did the Baranovs even know Susan Sarandon?

"What's in the boxes?" Teal asked, poking one.

"Stop that." Crane smacked his brother's hand, which saved Shel the trouble. "You take the top off, and there's a petit four inside."

"What the hell is a petit four?"

"It's a miniature cake."

"Oh. You can have mine, bro. I'll just take an extra baby burger instead. Listen, Shel, while I've got you alone, is it true you're giving dirt as wedding favors?"

Crane sighed, again saving Shel the trouble. "They're tulip bulbs, you ignoramus. The guests take them and plant them in the next week or so—they're a fall bulb, as everyone knows—and next spring a physical symbol of Shel and Alexandria's love will bloom."

"Yawn," Teal said.

"I think *my wife's* idea was charming."

"Okay, okay, don't burst a blood vessel, you big sissy. I still say they look like little clumps of dirt. You can dress them up in all the netting you want: they still look yuck."

"Oh, anything that's different looks 'yuck' to you, so be quiet."

"You know, since you got made first chair and moved to this place—"

"And knocked up your wife," Shel added helpfully.

"—you're more annoying than usual. And that's saying something!"

Crane ignored his brother's jibes. "Sheldon, are you all right? Do you need anything?" Crane pinched his brother and hissed, "We're his groomsmen, we're supposed to be asking questions like this."

"Yeah, do you need your back wubbed, wittle bitty groomey? How about a pony ride?"

He laughed, for the first time that day. "I'm fine, you morons. Well, moron, singular. I just came out to get some air. There's too many people fluttering around me inside."

"Like that Kathryn girl? She could flutter around me all she wants."

"Shut up, Teal, she's underage. And I guess . . ." He sighed. "I guess I better get used to it."

"Underage girls?"

"No, all the people." He sighed again.

Teal rolled his eyes. "Is this the part where we're supposed to cry for you because you're going to be stupidly wealthy for the rest of your life, Prince Sheldon?"

He didn't answer, instead, he changed the subject: "Did the rest of your sibs get here okay? Your folks?"

"Yup. Fourth row. They're in there right now, waiting to be impressed by the greatness that is us," Teal bragged.

"And my mother, for some unfathomable reason, wants to feel Jenny's stomach," Crane added.

"I'd feel Jenny's stomach," Teal leered.

Crane frowned at his brother. "You best get up there, then, Shel. Or wherever you're supposed to be."

"Yeah, don't want the king giving you a black eye. Did you see the size of that guy? And he's the one marrying you! I mean, you know. Not marrying you. Doing the ceremony."

"Alex wanted it that way." Shel shrugged. "It makes the, uh, coronation part easier."

"Ahhhhh. So they really just stick a crown on your head at the end and call it good?"

"The king does, yeah."

"Are you okay? You look kind of weird."

"My breakfast isn't agreeing with me. Why don't you guys go on in? I'll be right behind you."

Giving him identical doubtful looks, the twins left. Shel watched the bees—the palace employees—for a moment longer, then started the long death march toward the South end of the palace.

If he could have taken Alex without the title and the money and the employees and the royal protocol, he would have. Since he couldn't have her without all that other bullshit, he'd be the Prince of Alaska. But boy, oh boy, it would take some getting used to. Prince Sheldon! Ha!

It must be love, he thought, more than a little shocked. It must be! Because I would never—I could never have—but I can't live without her, either. Just the thought of it . . . he shivered again, and again, it had nothing to do with the weather.

"Wait! Oh, wait!"

He knew that voice, and instantly turned. There was the Princess of Alaska running toward him, *racing* toward him, her full white skirt caught up in her hands so she could navigate the turf better—he could see her matching shoes, pointy toes and diamond straps and all—he could see her hair jiggle, only the Baranov pearls keeping it from falling down past her shoulders in the dark cloud he knew well, so well he dreamed about it every night.

"It's okay," she gasped, finally reaching him. She pressed a hand to her bodice and fought for breath.

"Jeez, Alex, I don't think that dress is for, you know, running laps," he said mildly, but couldn't help grinning, he was so glad to see her.

"I mean . . . it's okay . . . you lasted longer . . . I don't want you to go . . . I'll hate it . . . but I understand . . ."

"Huh?"

"But I think . . . if you go . . . you're a coward . . ."

"I'm just getting some air, you nimrod! I'm not ducking out of the wedding." He looked around and observed that they were, for the moment, utterly alone. It was the perfect setting for an escape. "Uh, but I can see why you thought that. No, I was getting freaked out in there and came out here for a bit while I still could."

"Oh," she panted. "If I had . . . the energy . . . I'd be mortified . . . for thinking . . . the worst . . ."

"It's not like I haven't given you reason. Hey, do you need to sit down?"

"I'm . . . fine. That's—okay." She gulped a deep breath and swayed on her feet for a second, then seemed to recover from her mad dash across the lawn. "Well. Sorry. I saw you out the window and—and it's possible I jumped to conclusions."

"Trying to corral me before I could make my getaway, huh?" He looked her up and down. "My God, who could ever leave you?"

She dropped her skirts, covering her shoes, and he saw the dress in more detail now: off the shoulder, long sleeves, little white flowers sewn into the neckline, gigantic meringue skirt. Against the fall trees and the dying grass, she was the brightest thing on the grounds, the most beautiful.

His princess.

She smiled at him and reached up to see if her hair was in place; it was, secured firmly by the braids of pearls. Another set was around her neck, lustrous against her creamy skin: the Baranov pearls, inherited from her great-great grand-mother.

On her finger, another family heirloom gleamed: her late mother's jade engagement ring. The king had been so pleased that she'd accepted it—that Shel hadn't insisted on buying something himself—he'd had to leave the room.

In truth, Sheldon didn't care. If he was going to accept the royal thing, he would take all of it, not pick and choose as Christina tried to do. Alex came with the whole mess, and that was good enough for him.

She wanted to please her father by wearing her mom's

wedding jewelry? That was fine. In return, she had sworn never to make him eat artisanal cheese, and that was fine, too.

"I'm glad you're not running away," she said, "but it's bad luck to see me before the wedding."

"Hey, it wasn't my idea, sunshine. You're the one who came charging out of the palace like a royal pain."

"Oh, is that what I am?"

"Sure." He took her in his arms, carefully, mindful of the hair and the pearls and the dress and even the pointy shoes. "But in a few minutes, you'll be *my* royal pain. Her Highness Alexandria Baranov Rivers."

"Aw," she said, presenting her ripe, red mouth for a kiss. "Just call me Alex."

They kissed for a lovely long time and oh, it was sublime, she really was like something out of a fairy tale, she—

"Hey! Hey! You two! Cut the shit! You're gonna miss your own wedding!" The king was stomping toward them, Alex's bouquet of calla lilies—red and white and green—all mashed together in the king's fist. "I mean it! Let go! Both of you! Come on, we got a houseful of people waiting on you. Jesus Christ, will you *stop kissing for five seconds?*"

"Probably not," Shel said, and hugged his bride so hard, a Baranov pearl popped out of her headdress and rolled away in the grass, glossy cream against the dying green.

"I *will* turn the hose on you guys. Come on, you've lasted six months, it's only a couple hours more. Guys?" The king was pleading, brandishing Alex's bouquet like a sword, jabbing it at them like they were fighting dogs that needed to be separated. "Come on, I'm giving a royal command here. Let's just go inside and we can do this and then you can have a tiny hot dog. Guys? Okay? Guys?"

Here's a scintillating look at
WHO LOVES YA, BABY?
by Gemma Bruce,
available now from Brava!

The night was suddenly still. Cas peered into the woods again. He would swear someone was standing just inside the ring of trees, out of the moonlight. He rolled tight shoulders and cracked his neck. What the hell was he doing in Ex Falls, chasing burglars through the woods?

He snorted. His just desserts. He'd chased Julie through these woods more times than he could remember. And caught her. He smiled, forgetting where he was for a moment. He'd been pretty damn good at Cops and Robbers in those days. He'd been even better at Pirates.

A rustle in the trees. *Wind? No wind tonight.* Another rustle. Not a nocturnal animal, but a glimmer of white. All right, time to act, or he might still be standing here when the sun rose, and someone was bound to see him and by tomorrow night, it would be all over town that he had spent the night hiding behind a bush with an empty gun while the thieves got away.

Cas said a quick prayer that he was out of range and stepped away from the bush. He braced his feet in the standard two-handed shooting stance he learned from *NYPD Blue*, and aimed into the darkness. He sucked in his breath.

A figure stepped out to the edge of the trees. There was just enough light for Cas to see the really big handgun that was aimed at him.

The "freeze" he'd been about to yell froze on his lips.

"Freeze," said a deep voice from the darkness.

Hey, that was his line. He froze anyway, then yelped, "Police."

"Yeah. So drop the weapon and put your hands in the air. Slowly."

Cas dropped his gun. "No. I mean. Me. I'm the police."

"You're the sheriff?" A sound like strangling. "Why didn't you say so."

"I did. I was going to, but you—Who are you?"

"I'm the one who called you." The figure stepped into the moonlight. Not a thief, but an angel. Not an angel, but a vision that was the answer to every man's wet dream. A waterfall of long dark hair fell past slim shoulders and over a shimmering white shift that clung to every curve of a curvaceous body. His eyes followed the curves down to a pair of long, dynamite legs, lovely knees, tapering to . . . a pair of huge, untied work boots. He recognized the boots, they were his, but not the apparition that was wearing them.

He must be dreaming. That was it. It wouldn't be the first time he'd dreamed of Julie coming back to him. Her hair long and soft like this, hair a man could wrap his body in. A body that he could wrap his soul in. Mesmerized, Cas took a step toward her. She stepped back into the cover of the trees, disappearing into the darkness like a wraith. He took another step toward her and was stopped by a warning growl. His testicles climbed up to his rib cage. *Stay calm. It's just a dream.* Strange. He'd imagined Julie as many things— but never as a werewolf.

He barely registered the beast as it leapt through the air, flying toward him as if it had wings. *Time to wake up,* he told himself. *Now.*

He hit the ground and was pinned there by a ton of black fur and bad breath. The animal bared its teeth. Cas squeezed his eyes shut and felt a rough, wet tongue rasp over his face.

"Off, Smitty."

Cas heard the words, felt the beast being hauled off him. He slowly opened his eyes to find himself looking up at six legs: four, muscular and furry; two, muscular and sleek— and definitely female. He had to stop himself from reaching out to caress them.

Her companion growled and Cas yanked his eyes away to stare warily at the dog. He was pretty sure it was a dog. A really big dog.

"Never lower your firearm on a perp who might be armed." She waved the muzzle of her weapon in Cas's direction, then leaned over and picked up his .38 from the ground. She looked at it. "And maybe, next time, you should try loading this." She dropped it into his lap and heaved a sigh that lifted her shoulders and stretched the fabric of her shirt across her breasts. And Cas forgot about the dog, as he imagined sucking on the hard nipples that showed through the silk.

She stomped past him, shaking her head. The dog trotted after her.

Cas watched them—watched her—walk away, her hair trailing behind her, the work boots adding a hitch to her walk that swung her butt from side to side and set the fabric shifting and sliding against her body. And he wanted to touch her, slide his fingers inside the shift, and feel warm, firm flesh beneath his fingers. But mostly he wanted to touch her hair.

Halfway to the house, she paused and looked over her shoulder. "They're getting away," she said and continued toward the house.

After a stupefied second, he pushed himself off the ground. What was happening to him? He never thought about groping strange women, even magical ones like this one. He licked his lips, stuck his .38 in his jacket pocket and followed after her.

When he reached the porch, she was at the front door. So was the dog.

"Uh, miss . . . Ma'am? If you'd call off the dog, I could take down some information."

He saw a flick of her hand and he had to keep himself from diving for the bushes, but the dog merely padded past her into the house.

"Well, if you're not going to chase the thieves, you may as well come in," she said and turned to go inside.

"Wait," he cried.

She stopped mid-step.

"You might want to leave those boots on the porch."

She looked down at the work boots, sniffed, then wrinkled her nose. "Oh." She leaned over to pull them off.

Her ass tightened beneath the soft nightshirt, and Cas had a tightening response of his own. He shifted uncomfortably and stared at the mailbox until he got himself under control.

This was ridiculous. He should be used to this. For three months, women called him in all sorts of getups at all hours of the night. He was, after all, the town's most eligible bachelor. Actually he was the town's only eligible bachelor. None of them had the least affect on him. But this one knocked him right out of his socks. Made his dick throb, just looking at her. She might not be Julie, but she looked pretty damn good. He might as well find out who she was and what she was doing here—and how long she planned to stay.

"Coming?" she asked and let the screen door slam behind her.

Oh yeah, thought Cas, *I'm coming*.

Don't miss Dianne Castell's
newest contemporary romance
'TIL THERE WAS U
available now from Brava!

A woman in shorts, white blouse, barefoot and with a big purse slung over her shoulder was pulling something from the backseat. "The car's my rental, but I don't know who . . . Holy cow! Effie?"

"Who's Effie?"

"I . . . I'm not sure," he said to Rory as much as to himself as he took her in. Golden hair hanging free instead of bound up in some business do, a flimsy little blouse and . . . lots and lots of bare legs. No wonder she didn't want to lose her tan. Ryan ran his hand around the back of his neck. "I'm not sure at all and that's not good."

"I don't know who you're looking at, boy, but that gal is mighty fine."

California Effie he could handle, but this? Who the hell was this? She gave a final tug, the suitcase sliding all the way out, making her stumble backward and fall on the ground, the luggage landing on top of her.

Ryan rushed across the grass and picked up the luggage. Rory took Effie's arm and helped her up. "Are you okay, little lady? You should have waited for someone to help you with that thing. Could have squashed you flatter than a frog on the freeway."

"I'm fine, thank you," she said to Rory with a genuine smile, making Ryan suddenly want her to smile at him like that. "The porter at the airport must have jammed that suitcase in the back. Like a size twelve foot in a size nine shoe."

Rory's eyes twinkled. "Well, I'll be. Haven't heard that expression in a coon's age. A real country girl."

Effie laughed, and Ryan's insides did a little flip. She'd never laughed open and carefree like that before either. She said, "Born and raised in San Diego, but my grandparents lived on a farm. This place reminds me of it, sort of brings out that country girl you mentioned."

Ryan nudged the suitcase. "What the hell's in this thing? And where'd you get those clothes? You never dress like this."

She turned his way. "I only packed slacks. I hadn't planned on the blast furnace you all call the weather around here and being out in it. Thelma lent me clothes." Effie smoothed the blouse and shorts. "Wasn't that nice of her?"

"Thelma does not own short-shorts." Did she just say 'you all'?

"Rolled them up. And as for the luggage, I packed a fax machine and printer along with toner and paper so I can set up an office in the dining room. Thelma said it was okay with her and—"

"You packed office equipment?" Ryan watched a hint of breeze tease the wisps of blond hair curling in the humidity at her temples.

"You're the one who said the Landing was nothing like our office, that this place was rural."

"I didn't say they used stone tablets and smoke signals."

"Well, that's what you implied. All I know about Tennessee is that it has mountains and they filter whiskey through ten feet of sugar-maple charcoal." Effie shrugged. "One of my old boyfriends was a whiskey snob."

"I'm Rory O'Fallon," Rory said on a chuckle as he nodded at Ryan. "His daddy and happy as all get-out to meet you. The two of you together is damn interesting, I'll tell you that." He held out his hand to Effie.

Ryan felt as if he were seeing Effie for the first time, like when she'd come into his office all those months ago and knocked him on his ear. Trouble was, she was more beautiful now than then. He was certainly seeing parts of her he'd never seen before. Bare legs, bare arms, buttons open down the front of her blouse hinting at delectable cleavage where he suddenly wanted to bury his face. Shit!

Why couldn't he work with the big fat guy down the hall and have him along now? Because the big fat guy wasn't half the architect Effie Wilson was.

Rory hitched his chin toward the river. "We've got whatever office equipment you need right down at the landing. Help yourself anytime, though cell phones don't work for spit in these parts." He grinned. "The crew will sure appreciate having you around, give them something nice and pretty to look at and brighten their day. Hope you don't mind a wolf whistle or two. They don't mean nothing by it, just a little appreciation for the finer things in life."

Did Effie blush? Ryan had never seen her do that. Made her eyes greener, her hair blonder, her skin shimmer. No way was he letting her go to any damn docks.

Okay, this great idea to bring her along so they could work together was not his best lifetime idea. In fact, it sucked. He'd thought things would be the same as in the office; he could handle Effie in a suit and buttoned up. Except she sure as hell wasn't buttoned up now. He had to get rid of her, just like he told Rory he would. "Afraid she won't get that far, Dad. Effie's leaving in the morning."

"I am?"

"There's no need for you to be here. I've reconsidered."

She folded her arms and glared at him. "Well, bully for you."

"I can take care of everything."

"Like designing the mall by yourself." Her foot nudged the luggage by his feet. Cute toes with dark red painted toenails. "I don't think so, and I didn't haul all this crap across the continent to just pack it up again and leave without using it."

She tied together her shirttails with a decisive yank, showing her narrow waist and giving Ryan a quick peek at her navel—her navel pierced by a little gold ring—as she made the knot.

His mouth went dry; his head wobbled on his neck. He had to swallow before he could speak. How could she make a baggy shirt of Thelma's look like this? "What happened to 'I'm a businesswoman, a California girl?' What about your cat and sushi?"

"What happened to me owing you for the shoes and the mall plans?"

Rory's eyes widened a fraction. "Ryan, this Ryan, bought you shoes?"

Effie nodded and did a mischievous wiggle with her eyebrows. "And they're Italian."

Thank God she didn't wiggle anything else.

Take a peek at JoAnn Ross's
sizzling romantic novella
"Cajun Heat"
from the upcoming
BAYOU BAD BOYS
anthology available next month from Brava!

It was funny how life turned out. Who'd have thought that a girl who'd been forced to buy her clothes in the Chubbettes department of the Tots to Teens Emporium, the very same girl who'd been a wallflower at her senior prom, would grow up to have men pay to get naked with her?

It just went to show, Emma Quinlan considered, as she ran her hands down her third bare male back of the day, that the American dream was alive and well and living in Blue Bayou, Louisiana.

Not that she'd dreamed that much of naked men back when she'd been growing up.

She'd been too sheltered, too shy, and far too inhibited. Then there'd been the weight issue. Photographs showed that she'd been a cherubic infant, the very same type celebrated on greeting cards and baby food commercials.

Then she'd gone through a "baby fat" stage. Which, when she was in the fourth grade, resulted in her being sent off to a fat camp where calorie cops monitored every bite that went into her mouth and did surprise inspections of the cabins, searching out contraband. One poor calorie criminal had been caught with packages of Gummi Bears hidden beneath a loose floorboard beneath his bunk. Years later, the memory of his frightened eyes as he struggled to plod his way through a punishment lap of the track was vividly etched in her mind.

The camps became a yearly ritual, as predictable as the return of swallows to the Louisiana Gulf Coast every August on their fall migration.

For six weeks during July and August, every bite Emma put in her mouth was monitored. Her days were spent doing calisthenics and running around the oval track and soccer field; her nights were spent dreaming of crawfish jambalaya, chicken gumbo, and bread pudding.

There were rumors of girls who'd trade sex for food, but Emma had never met a camper who'd actually admitted to sinking that low, and since she wasn't the kind of girl any of the counselors would've hit on, she'd never had to face such a moral dilemma.

By the time she was fourteen, Emma realized that she was destined to go through life as a "large girl." That was also the year that her mother—a petite blonde, whose crowning achievement in life seemed to be that she could still fit into her size zero wedding dress fifteen years after the ceremony—informed Emma that she was now old enough to shop for back-to-school clothes by herself.

"You are so lucky!" Emma's best friend, Roxi Dupree, had declared that memorable Saturday afternoon. "My mother is so old-fashioned. If she had her way, I'd be wearing calico like Half-Pint in *Little House on the Prairie!*"

Roxi might have envied what she viewed as Emma's shopping freedom, but she hadn't seen the disappointment in Angela Quinlan's judicious gaze when Emma had gotten off the bus from the fat gulag, a mere two pounds thinner than when she'd been sent away.

It hadn't taken a mind reader to grasp the truth—that

Emma's former beauty queen mother was ashamed to go clothes shopping with her fat teenage daughter.

"Uh, sugar?"

The deep male voice shattered the unhappy memory. *Bygones*, Emma told herself firmly.

"Yes?"

"I don't want to be tellin' you how to do your business, but maybe you're rubbing just a touch hard?"

Damn. She glanced down at the deeply tanned skin. She had such a death grip on his shoulders. "I'm so sorry, Nate."

"No harm done," he said, the south Louisiana drawl blending appealingly with his Cajun French accent. "Though maybe you could use a bit of your own medicine. You seem a tad tense."

"It's just been a busy week, what with the Jean Lafitte weekend coming up."

Liar. The reason she was tense was not due to her days, but her recent sleepless nights.

She danced her fingers down his bare spine. And felt the muscles of his back clench.

"I'm sorry," she repeated, spreading her palms outward.

"No need to apologize. That felt real good. I was going to ask you a favor, but since you're already having a tough few days—"

"Don't be silly. We're friends, Nate. Ask away."

She could feel his chuckle beneath her hands. "That's what I love about you, *chere*. You agree without even hearing what the favor is."

He turned his head and looked up at her, affection warming his Paul Newman blue eyes. "I was supposed to pick someone up at the airport this afternoon, but I got a call that these old windows I've been trying to find for a remodel job are goin' on auction in Houma this afternoon, and—"

"I'll be glad to go to the airport. Besides, I owe you for getting your brother to help me out."

If it hadn't been for Finn Callahan's detective skills, Emma's louse of an ex-husband would've gotten away with absconding with all their joint funds. Including the money she'd socked away in order to open her Every Body's Beautiful day spa. Not only had Finn—a former FBI agent—not charged her his going rate, Nate insisted on paying for the weekly massage the doctor had prescribed after he'd broken his shoulder falling off a scaffolding.

"You don't owe me a thing. Your ex is pond scum. I was glad to help put him away."

Having never been one to hold grudges, Emma had tried not to feel gleeful when the news bulletin about her former husband's arrest for embezzlement and tax fraud had come over her car radio.

"So, what time is the flight, and who's coming in?"

"It gets in at five thirty-five at Concourse D. It's a Delta flight from L.A."

"Oh?" Her heart hitched. Oh, please. She cast a quick, desperate look into the adjoining room at the voodoo altar, draped in Barbie-pink tulle, that Roxi had set up as packaging for her "hex appeal" love spell business. Don't let it be—

"It's Gabe."

Damn. Where the hell was voodoo power when you needed it?

"Well." She blew out a breath. "That's certainly a surprise."

That was an understatement. Gabriel Broussard had been so eager to escape Blue Bayou, he'd hightailed it out of town without so much as a good-bye.

Not that he'd owed Emma one.

The hell he didn't. Okay. Maybe she did hold a grudge. But only against men who'd kissed her silly, felt her up until she'd melted into a puddle of hot, desperate need, then disappeared from her life.

Unfortunately, Gabriel hadn't disappeared from the planet. In fact, it was impossible to go into a grocery store without seeing his midnight blue eyes smoldering from the cover of some sleazy tabloid. There was usually some barely clad female plastered to him.

Just last month, an enterprising photographer with a telescopic lens had captured him supposedly making love to his co-star on the deck of some Greek shipping tycoon's yacht. The day after that photo hit the newsstands, splashed all over the front of the *Enquirer*, the actress's producer husband had filed for divorce.

Then there'd been this latest scandal with Tamara the prairie princess . . .

"Guess you've heard what happened," Nate said.

Emma shrugged. "I may have caught something on *Entertainment Tonight* about it." And had lost sleep for the past three nights imagining what, exactly, constituted kinky sex.

"Gabe says it'll blow over."

"Most things do, I suppose." It's what people said about Hurricane Ivan. Which had left a trail of destruction in its wake.

"Meanwhile, he figured Blue Bayou would be a good place to lie low."

"How lucky for all of us," she said through gritted teeth.

"You sure nothing's wrong, *chere*?"

"Positive." She forced a smile. It wasn't his fault that his best friend had the sexual morals of an alley cat. "All done."

"And feeling like a new man." He rolled his head onto his shoulders. Then he retrieved his wallet from his back pocket and handed her his Amex card. "You definitely have magic hands, Emma, darlin'."

"Thank you." Those hands were not as steady as they should have been as she ran the card. "I guess Gabe's staying at your house, then?"

"I offered. But he said he'd rather stay out at the camp."

Terrific. Not only would she be stuck in a car with the man during rush hour traffic, she was also going to have to return to the scene of the crime.

"You sure it's no problem? He can always rent a car, but bein' a star and all, as soon as he shows up at the Hertz counter, his cover'll probably be blown."

She forced a smile she was a very long way from feeling. "Of course, it's no problem."

"Then why are you frowning?"

"I've got a headache coming on." A two-hundred-and-and-ten pound Cajun one. "I'll take a couple aspirin and I'll be fine."

"You're always a damn sight better than fine, *chere*." His grin was quick and sexy, without the seductive overtones that had always made his friend's smile so dangerous.

She could handle this, Emma assured herself as she locked up the spa for the day. An uncharacteristic forty-five minutes early, which had Cal Marchand, proprietor of Cal's Cajun Café across the street checking his watch in surprise.

The thing to do was to just pull on her big girl underpants, drive into New Orleans, and get it over with. Gabriel Broussard might be *People* magazine's sexiest man alive. He might have seduced scores of women all over the world, but the man *Cosmo* readers had voted the pirate they'd most like to be held prisoner on a desert island with was, after all, just a man. Not that different from any other.

Besides, she wasn't the same shy, tongue-tied, small-town bayou girl she'd been six years ago. She'd lived in the city; she'd gotten married only to end up publicly humiliated by a man who turned out to be slimier than swamp scum.

It hadn't been easy, but she'd picked herself up, dusted herself off, divorced the dickhead, as Roxi loyally referred to him, started her own business and was a dues paying member of Blue Bayou's Chamber of Commerce.

She'd even been elected deputy mayor, which was, admittedly, an unpaid position, but it did come with the perk of riding in a snazzy convertible in the Jean Lafitte Day parade. Roxi, a former Miss Blue Bayou, had even taught her a beauty queen wave.

She'd been fired in the crucible of life. She was intelligent, tough, and had tossed off her nice girl Catholic upbringing after the dickhead dumped her for another woman. A bimbo who'd applied for a loan to buy a pair of D cup boobs so she could win a job as a cocktail waitress at New Orleans' Coyote Ugly Saloon.

Emma might not be a tomb raider like Lara Croft, or an international spy with a to-kill-for wardrobe and a trunkful of glamorous wigs like *Alias*'s Sydney Bristow, but this new, improved Emma Quinlan could take names and kick butt right along with the rest of those fictional take-charge females.

And if she were the type of woman to hold a grudge, which she wasn't, she assured herself yet again, the butt she'd most like to kick belonged to Blue Bayou bad boy Gabriel Broussard.